THE RANCH

You're Hurting Me

NINA K. JOHNSON

NINA K. JOHNSON

ARPress
45 Dan Road, Suite 36
Canton, MA 02021
Hotline: 1(800) 220-7660
Fax: 1(855) 752-6001

Ordering Information:
Quantity sales. Special discounts are available on quantity purchases by corporations, associations, and others. For details, contact the publisher at the address above.

Printed in the United States of America.

Library of Congress Control Number
ISBN-13:   Paperback   979-8-89389-044-0
                eBook   979-8-89389-045-7

Rev. date: 03/23/2019

ANNA

Anna was the daughter of Samson Creed Carter and Patricia Violet Carter, owners of one of the largest ranches in Texas. The Carters were the third generation to live and work on the The Ranch.

When deciding the name and brand for their ranch, Anna's great-great-grandfather said, "It's The Ranch. That's what we've always called it. That's what everyone calls it." That settled it. From then on their property would be known as The Ranch.

Anna was standing at the entrance of The Ranch Church. The church was filled, but no one seemed to notice her. She knew everyone most of them her whole life. But the two people most important to her, she didn't see. Her parents could not be here. Anna had been very close to her parents. She was trying hard to think of what her dad might have said to her at this moment, but she couldn't think. She really wanted/ needed to talk to her mother. There was so much she wanted to ask her.

She knew it would have pleased her mother that she was wearing the traditional gown that her mother and her grandmother wore on their wedding day. Each bride had added their own individual touch. Her grandmother had added pearls to the bodice of the gown; her mother had continued with the pearls, adding them to the skirt and train. Anna had added a thin twenty-four-carat gold thread to accent the dress. The gold not only accented the dress, but the gold accented Anna's porcelain white skin and her golden hair. Anna looked like a golden goddess.

She missed them terribly, today more than ever. She stepped back and started remembering.

* * * * *

Anna was her daddy's sidekick. She loved him and everything about his life. Before she was even walking, when he was on a horse, she was with him. If he was in a piece of farm equipment, she was in the cab with him. Her mom was always there as well, recording Anna's life. Anna was happy now more than ever to have the albums and videos. Anna and her mother spent their mornings together. Very little was allowed to interfere.

As Anna got older her mother put her in ballet, tap, gymnastics, baton twirling, cheer, swim classes. Her mom never just dropped her off, she was one of the mothers that stayed throughout. She was always amazed how quickly Anna picked up on the instruction and imitated the movements. Her mother afforded her every opportunity that might broaden Anna's world. Anna loved it all. Her mother loved shopping and would spend her afternoons shopping while Anna was with her daddy on The Ranch. Whatever her mom bought for her to wear, Anna wore and loved it. Samson and Trisha knew they were blessed. Their little Anna was happy. She loved to learn new things, and she was enjoying life.

Samson Creed came from a long line of teachers, and he was a natural. When Anna accompanied him, he broke down everything they were observing or doing into steps where she could understand it all. He was rewarded with her joy of learning and accomplishing the things he loved.

Anna started walking before her first birthday, but her daddy couldn't wait until her birthday. He brought her a pony home that night. She named her pony Daisy. She and her mother would weave daisies to hang around Daisy's neck. Her mother would say, "We've got to dress Daisy up," and they would both giggle. The sound of them giggling was heard every day around The Ranch. Samson listened for it, and the ranch hands listened for it. It was a happy sound that just made them smile.

Anna's life was filled with love. Besides her parents, Jewel, who was the cook in their home, loved to have Anna in the kitchen with her. It was the same in the kitchen as everywhere else in Anna's life. Jewel never had to tell her or show her anything more than once. The two were always heard singing gospel songs and whipping up something sweet smelling.

When Anna was ten, many things happened that would affect the rest of her life. She was in the kitchen with Jewel, and Anna thought she could hear a puppy whining. She knew all the cow dogs stayed down around the bunkhouses. The cow dogs were specially bred and trained, and they worked hard right alongside the ranch hands. They were never around the main house. She asked Jewel if she heard it, but Jewel was busy doing three different things getting the meal ready. Anna wondered out onto the back porch, and she could hear the puppy better. The porch went all the way around the house, and there were steps down at each door. She went down the stairs. Now she knew, it was a puppy in pain. Lots of things happens on The Ranch, and Anna thought maybe a big cat might have gotten one of the dogs. Anna was still small enough to get under the house, so she crawled under the porch. She wanted to help. It took her a moment for her eyes to adjust. The sun hadn't gone down but would soon be pitch-black. She thought she spotted the puppy. It was pitch-black. Well, that ruled out the cow dogs. They were black and white, mainly white. Maybe it was a neighbor's or someone might have just dropped it off. People tended to drop off unwanted animals. Anna could never figure out why they would just leave the animals by the side of the road.

Her dad always had a place for the rescues. If there were already too many at one bunkhouse, he would take them to another. There were four bunkhouses on The Ranch. Anna crawled in further and could see the size of the dog. It was easily three times bigger than her. Then she realized it was a wolf and it was trying to have pups but there was a problem. Well, she knew how to deliver cows, she figured she could do this. She started talking quietly to the wolf just like she did the cows. She was telling her that she could help, that everything would be okay as she had the experience. The wolf seemed to calm down. Anna lay down beside the wolf, only her feet were at the wolf's head and Anna's head was behind the wolf's back feet. The next thing Anna heard was the wolf starting to whine. She put her long arms inside the wolf and turned the pup for it to come out. Anna petted the wolf and said, "One more push." Sure enough the wolf whined and pushed, and with Anna's help the pup slid out. Anna handed the pup to the wolf. Anna was so caught up in watching how carefully the wolf cleaned and cared for her pup that she was surprised when the wolf started whining. Anna was still in position and was just thinking that this always happens. Her dad called it the birth. Then another pup dropped out. Anna handed the pup to her mother, then waited for the afterbirth and climbed out from under the porch.

Anna went into the back door. She knew she was dirty and smelly. She dropped her clothes in the mud room and made a mad dash up the back stairs and took a quick shower. When she got back to the kitchen, Jewel was still busy. Anna took a gallon of milk out of one of the refrigerators and a large bowl out of the cabinet. Jewel didn't seem to notice. Anna went back out and under the porch. This time she had also brought old sheets. She set down the milk and bowl. She laid a path with the sheets from the side of the steps to Wolf. That was what she was going to call this large black wolf. She went back for the milk and bowl, then crawled on the sheet to keep from getting dirty. She had talked quietly to Wolf the whole time. She set the large bowl by Wolf's head and poured the gallon of milk in the bowl. Wolf lapped it up. Anna talked with Wolf some more until she heard her dad and the foreman coming in for supper. She crawled out and ran into the mud room and cleaned up.

The minute she saw her dad, she knew something had happened. She was right. He had a ninety-nine-year lease on the few acres of property he didn't own in the farthest north mile section line. The grandchildren that inherited needed cash, so they sold the property out from under him. The new owner wasn't going to honor the lease. She knew her dad had tens of thousands of acres and miles and miles of fence line. The nearest neighbors lived twenty miles away. He didn't even use the property. It was more about security. He felt if he owned the whole section, it was easier to fence and maintain security. Plus he was mad about how secretive the whole sale had been done. He was going tomorrow to meet the new owner.

When supper was over, Anna helped clear the table. The adults were still talking, and she wanted to get some scraps for Wolf. She liked helping Jewel as Jewel was always singing and happy. Sometimes she messed up the words of the songs, but she would just keep right on singing and laughing. There was a slop jar for the pigs. It was just a pot that had scraps put in it for the pigs. Anna volunteered to take it out. Jewel agreed, saying, "It isn't too full. You ought to be able to handle it, little one. Thank you."

Anna went out the back door and crawled under the porch. It was dark now, but her eyes adjusted. She talked quietly to Wolf while she got the large bowl. She filled the bowl with scraps and crawled back to Wolf. Anna loved the wolf pups but didn't make any movements toward them. She knew all animals were defensive of their young. Thinking, she added, except some humans. She was remembering Johnny, a new boy in her class this year. She tried to be friends with him, but he seemed scared all the time. One time she even whispered to him, "School is a safe place." She started sharing her lunch with him when she saw his parents had sent only crackers. He made sure to sit with her. She would pull a whole sack lunch out of her sack for him. It was amazing that no one ever noticed. Then he came to school with a long-sleeve shirt on when the temperature was 102 degrees. She told him she would show him how to roll up his sleeves and make short sleeves.

He said his stepdad told him he had to wear this shirt and not show the burns on his arms. He said, "I'm only telling you because I know you won't tell. It won't matter. We will probably move. My stepdad lost his job."

Anna quickly said, "He can work for my dad. My dad hires people all the time to help on The Ranch."

Johnny said, "My dad thinks he's too good to work on a ranch. He thinks he has to have a job with an air conditioner. I would love to work on The Ranch."

Anna said, "When you are sixteen, you come to The Ranch. I'll make sure my dad hires you. You would love it."

The next three days she told Johnny all about The Ranch. He asked her all sorts of questions. It was the first time she had seen him show any interest.

Anna heard her mom calling. She crawled out from under the porch wondering if she would ever see Johnny again.

"Why did his daddy burn him with cigarettes?" she had heard another boy say that after Johnny was gone.

"Where was his mother?" she heard another kid ask.

Someone said, "Sitting right there, smoking."

Anna had run to the bathroom crying. When her teacher came to check on her, she said she needed to go home, that she felt bad. "Please call my mother."

Anna told her parents about Johnny the minute she got home. Her dad had come in as soon as he learned she was sick and Trisha was headed to pick her up. He was waiting when they walked in the front door. Anna burst into tears, telling her parents all about Johnny and what she had overheard the boys say. They tried to console her. Finally, Samson said he would look into the family and try to find them and help Johnny. That was the only thing that would console her.

She was sad as she walked through the house. Her mother asked what was wrong, and she said she was thinking of Johnny. Her mom told her to get ready for bed and she would come in and talk until Anna fell asleep. Thinking of Johnny made tears come to Trisha's eyes. Samson had looked into the man and found out he was a bully with a hot temper. That's why he lost his job. Samson had security track him down. He was going to try to get Johnny out of that house. Security came back and reported that the man Samson had them tracking was in jail for killing his wife. Samson wanted to know about the boy. They said he moved back in with his biological Dad, and Johnny seemed very happy at home and at school. They told Anna, and she seemed glad and also reminded her dad that when Johnny was sixteen she had promised him a job.

Already trying to run the ranch, her daddy loved it!

Her mom came in, and they talked about Johnny and other kids that were in bad situations. It worked out for Johnny, but it doesn't always work out. Her mother told her of two organizations that she and Samson donated their time and money to.

She said, "Your dad and I think it's time for you to start going with us to these functions and helping firsthand."

Anna was so excited. She loved the idea. Her mother left her to dream. Right before she went to sleep she remembered she hadn't told her parents about Wolf and Wolf's pups.

The next day her dad went over to the neighboring ranch. When he came back home Anna was under the porch. She could hear her parents talking in the kitchen. They often sat in the kitchen and had coffee and cookies or something else sweet Jewel had made. She could tell by her dad's voice that he was angry.

The fur on Wolf stood up like a cats, but before she could growl, Anna started talking low and comforting her. Today Wolf let the puppies explore Anna. Anna loved every minute but made sure the pups were back close to their mother where they could eat. She crawled out, and there stood both her parents.

Her mom said, "What are you doing under the porch?"

Anna said excitedly, "There is a wolf living under our porch, and I helped her deliver her pups." Anna looked at her parents and thought they looked like they might die of fright.

Samson bent down and looked under the porch, but he was too big to get in the crawl space. He let his eyes adjust and sure enough saw a black mama wolf and two black pups.

The mama wolf growled low, and Anna said, "Daddy, she doesn't know you. You know how protective mothers are!" as she pointed to her mom.

He burst out laughing. He couldn't help himself. How in the world was he going to handle this? He began by saying, "Anna, wolves are not pets."

She said, "I know. She will leave when her pups get old enough."

Anna was in bed and started thinking. Her dad was mad before he knew about the wolves. What had he been saying about the new neighbor? She was remembering he was saying that he had stopped by the feedstore and Bart, the owner, was telling him how the new neighbor came in bragging, "Best ranch, best herd, best ranch hands—that kind of thing. Before you know it, I'll be the owner of the biggest ranch in Texas."

Bart said, "I have a bad feeling about him. We both know that land isn't good grazing land and the buildings need a lot of work."

Anna's dad had answered back, "That why I let it sit all these years."

Bart said, "The minute he left, I called my brother Brett (president of the bank) to make sure his check cleared. He had the same bad feeling about the man. Brett said, 'The man has no banking history.' Brett heard the man's wife drown, and that's how he bought the land. She was one of the heirs, and he bought the others out for pennies on the dollar. I'm just saying be careful. Oh yeah, I forgot to tell you, the last thing the man said was, who the hell did you think you were naming your place The Ranch. There were plenty of ranches just as big or bigger. Someone needs to bring you down a peg."

Anna thought over the conversation and thought again of Johnny. This new neighbor sounded a lot like Johnny's dad. That wasn't good.

The next morning Anna's dad told her he wanted her to spend the morning with him. After breakfast they went to his office. He told Anna that he wanted her to start helping with the ledgers. He got out a huge ledger from the massive safe and opened it.

Anna said, "I'm going to love this," and he answered, "Me too."

So when Anna was ten, Wolf became her companion. She met Johnny and heard his story of bullying and abuse and started being active in organizations that empowered victims. She got a new neighbor, and her dad hired full-time security. For some reason she had a feeling those two things were connected. Her daddy started teaching her how to keep The Ranch ledgers. When she was thirteen, he turned them over to her. He never again checked her numbers. He knew they were correct.

Anna's parents were a part of every aspect of her life, and she loved every minute of it. In her junior high and high school years, she received every academic honor and was elected as queen of every organization. Her classmates loved her. Her junior and senior year, her picture was on over twenty pages in the yearbook. That was only her school honors. She received many awards outside of school in community organizations. Her parents were always, always there. She wanted her mommy and daddy now. When her heart should have been full, her heart was breaking.

Anna loved her parents and The Ranch. She loved every aspect of her ranch life. That was one of the reasons she had known that she wanted to be a veterinarian. She had taken classes for college credit in her junior and senior years in high school just to be able to be accepted to the College of Veterinary Science sooner. A minute after graduating high school, she was off to Texas A & M to begin her classes. Anna enjoyed every minute of her classes! Her classmates referred to her as the Girly Girl. They had only seen her on campus, and she was always dressed to the nines. Her mother had picked and packed her wardrobe just as she had done all of Anna's life. Anna knew her mother would pick whatever was needed for the occasion. Anna loved the things her mother picked and was happy to wear them.

The first time her class went out to deliver calves, Anna surprised them all. She was dressed in a set of work clothes she had worn often on The Ranch. To complete the outfit she had on her work hat, gloves, and boots. She stepped up and help deliver one calf after another. Anna was unaware of what her classmates were doing, but she was on alert if a calf was struggling no matter who was delivering the calf. She found out later that no one had helped deliver as many calves as Anna. But that had never been her objective. She looked at things from her dad's point of view—the more healthy the calves, the better for The Ranch. All her calves were doing well. She had also helped a few classmates whose calves were struggling to get them up and breathing. One classmate finally asked Anna how old she had been when she started delivering calves. Anna answered, "Two years old." They all laughed as if she had made a joke. But the veterinarian in charge of the project knew she was telling the truth.

The more knowledge she obtained the better for The Ranch. She would often excitedly call her parents to tell them anything she learned that they could implement immediately on the ranch. Sometimes she called them multiple times a day to tell them what was going on in her life. They would stop everything and take her calls. Anna didn't know that her parents had full-time security on her. They had protected her all her life, and they would continue to do so. Anna's parents furnished her with The Ranch limousine and driver even though Anna had a driver's license and pickup she drove on The Ranch. She never questioned her parents about the car and driver. Now she was thinking maybe she should have. Why was there a full-time staff of security on The Ranch? What were they afraid of?

JOE JR.

Joe Jr. stood at the front of The Ranch Church. This was actually the first time he had ever been in The Ranch Church. He had never been invited to any of the private services that had been held in the church. He was actually older than his bride; and his father, who insisted everyone call him Papa Joe, had sent him away from the community when he was in high school. So even though he and his bride were raised in a small ranching community, their paths had really never crossed. He had been sent away over dating a girl Papa Joe didn't approve. Ironically, now Papa Joe had insisted he come home and had even chosen the girl he was to not only date but marry.

Joe Jr. was so furious. He was blinded to the fact that he had a beautiful and accomplished bride waiting at the church door to walk down the aisle to him. Papa Joe also insisted that Joe Jr. back the story that Papa Joe had led the whole ranching community to believe. That story was that Joe Jr. had gone on to the University (Papa Joe never specified which university) and had completed his graduate degree and was now working on his doctorate. Papa Joe had refined his stories about Joe Jr. through the years. He was very convincing. Once Papa Joe was asked, "What university?" Papa Joe replied, "The University." The person asking the question knew what Papa Joe was implying. If his son went there, it meant it was the best in every way. "The University" and no other could be in the same category.

In reality Joe Jr. did attend a university and successfully joined a fraternity but flunked out without completing his freshman year. The truth was Joe Jr. lost the only two women he had ever loved because of his papa Joe. He had left when he was a senior because he knew if he didn't obey, Papa Joe would kill his girl. He had known since he was ten years old what Papa Joe was capable of if anyone crossed him or even thought about crossing him.

When Joe Jr. was ten years old, his grandpa Joe died. Papa Joe took his mother and him to the funeral. Joe Jr. could remember his mother waking him up that morning. It was still dark outside. She was all dressed in black including a black hat. She dressed him in all black. He remembered thinking where did the clothes come from. He had never seen them, and they were new. It was the first new clothes he had ever had, and when he walked out to the car, his dad had on all black. His dad must have cleaned the car. It was shiny as new. That was the morning that his dad announced that from now on he was to be addressed as Papa Joe. Joe Jr.'s mother laughed and said, "That would be silly for Joe Jr. and I to call you Papa Joe." Papa Joe pinched her arm until she stopped laughing and tears were in her eyes.

In the car Joe Jr. slept. He woke up needing to go to the bathroom. Papa Joe said, "We are not stopping. You need to just hold it. I want to get there before dark, and I will get there before dark." His mom had said she needed to stop as well, and Papa Joe slapped her and said, "Don't ever side against me, not even with your son." His mother had brought lunch, and she emptied out a container into another and handed Joe Jr. the empty container when Papa Joe was occupied with talking about some huge house they were passing. Joe Jr. mouthed, "I'm sorry," to his mother. He knew exactly what to do, and when he was through, he closed the lid on the container tightly. The windows were down, and the warm wind made him sleepy. Joe Jr. fell back to sleep. He woke up when the car stopped. He thought they were at his grandpa's, but they had pulled off the road under a shade tree. His dad, Papa Joe, pulled him out of the car by his shirt collar and said, "Now is the time to go to the bathroom, and we will eat." Joe Jr was really glad he needed to go again. He didn't know what Papa Joe might have done if he didn't go. While his mother was fixing lunch, he quietly emptied the container and put it back into the back floorboard. He made sure to scoot in under the seat where it couldn't be seen. The minute Papa Joe finished eating, he started the car and pulled back on the road.

Joe Jr. heard Papa Joe say, "Our ship has finally come in. We will no longer have to live in a shack and wear old clothes."

His mother said, "What are you talking about? Grandpa didn't have anything of value. Our house is better than the one he lives in. Plus whatever he has will be split between my brothers and sisters and I. That's five ways."

Papa Joe said, "You just hold on to your hat and let Papa Joe take care of everything."

Two days later all his mother's brothers and sisters and their spouses and kids were leaving with their pockets and pickups full.

His mother said, "I don't understand you. Where did you get all the money you paid my family?"

Papa Joe yelled, "Women, you are so stupid! I sold our place, furniture and all!" He looked so proud!

Joe Jr.'s mother looked sick. His mother said, "Where are we going to live?"

Papa Joe was really fed up that his wife couldn't see how he was going to take care of them. He slapped her and said, "Can't you see? I'm going to build us a big ranch house and we will raise cattle."

His mother was crying now, but she got up enough backbone to say, "How?"

Papa Joe said, "I will get the money from the bank! I will mortgage this land!"

The next morning Papa Joe drove into Dallas and filed the deed on the land that all the siblings had signed. Then he went to the first bank he saw and walked in like he owned the world and mortgaged the property. Papa Joe started building a house and buying cattle. By the time Joe Jr. was thirteen, he knew Papa Joe bought everything on credit. He borrowed from one bank to pay another. Even when his ranch started generating money, Papa Joe only paid as little as he could get by paying.

Something else happened when Joe Jr. was thirteen. He had seen Papa Joe pinch and beat his mother any time his mother tried to question him about the money. She tried many times to try to make things balance in her mind and never had any success. Joe Jr. had been out riding their ranch all day and was tired after supper. He went on to bed. Something woke him up. It sounded like someone was in the room with him. He lay very still. He realized it was his mother and Papa Joe fighting once again. His mother must have been in her bathroom. She liked to take long baths. She used a heavy-scented lilac bath oil. She said it relaxes her. Joe Jr. had heard them fighting before when she is in the bathroom, but he would usually only hear her voice. Tonight Papa Joe must have walked into her bathroom because Joe Jr. could hear him just as plain. She was saying that she didn't understand why he wouldn't help her two sisters. They just wanted money to help pay their way to visit them.

Papa Joe said, "They can get a job! Your sisters can get a job. I gave those bums money, and they celebrated until it was gone. I'm not giving them one penny. The state can support them. I will never…" Then Joe Jr. could tell by the noises that Papa Joe was going back into the bedroom but he turned around and said, "Have you already given some of *my* money to them? I can tell by looking at you that you have." There was struggling, and Papa Joe was yelling, "*How much?*" There was the sound of more struggling. Then Joe Jr. heard Papa Joe leave the bathroom.

Joe Jr. stayed up all night, but he never heard his mother leave the bathroom. The next morning when Joe Jr. went down to breakfast, he was wide awake. There were two ladies in the kitchen. They brought breakfast out to him, and he asked them where his mother was. They said they were very sorry, but his papa Joe would be home soon to talk to him. He felt he was going to throw up the breakfast he just ate. He was thinking, *If they get a divorce, I am going with my mother. Even if I have to live in a shack.*

When Papa Joe came in, he took the stairs two at a time to find Joe Jr. in his bedroom. He shut the door and said, "Your mother committed suicide last night. She was always weak. She walked out to the front pond and drowned. She was very weak and stupid. I hope you will be nothing like her." Papa Joe walked out of the room, and Joe Jr. threw up. He knew Papa Joe killed his mother. He had heard it.

The sheriff's deputy put "suspected suicide" on his report after listening to Papa Joe about how she was weak and how her sisters were putting pressure on her for money. He blamed the sisters for expecting her to support them. He said they wanted money to visit and then he would have been stuck with those freeloaders. He blamed the sisters for turning out to be nobodies living off the government dime. When the reality was her sisters' husbands were doing well. They just wanted money to come see her and check on her.

Once again Joe Jr was dressed in a new black suit. He had locked the door of his room and cried. When he was finished crying, he promised himself he would ruin Papa Joe's life. The sisters did come to the funeral, and they told the sheriff deputy that in their hearts they knew Papa Joe killed her. He told them that what they said would be included in his report, but there was no evidence pointing that direction. He asked them if they had asked their sister for money, and they had said that they had. They wanted to come visit and check on her.

The coroner's report was delivered to the sheriff's deputy six days after the cremation. The coroner's report read, "Observed bubbles smelling of lilac in and around female's mouth. Stomach also contained water with lilac oil. No water consistent with the pond water was found in female's mouth or stomach. Female did not die in the pond. Suspect foul play."

Papa Joe had called the coroner's office to see when the report would be finished. He was at the sheriff's office waiting to take the deputy out for lunch when the report arrived. Papa Joe slipped the report in his briefcase. No one noticed.

Chapter 1

Today Anna stood at the doors of The Ranch Church, the only church she had attended since her birth. Her mother liked to tell her she had attended it even before she was born. When her mother was pregnant with Anna, she attended the church faithfully. Her mother had told her many times that she had requested the minister preach on faith, hope, and love during her nine months of pregnancy. The minister hadn't let her down.

She wished her mother was with her today. She felt so uncertain. She had never felt uncertain in her life. She wished both her parents had been here today. She had no family to talk her uncertainty through with. No family to advise her. She was so certain three days ago, then came one wedding event after another, and each event made her question her decision to marry. Anna looked down the aisle. She didn't see her groom. She saw Marion and Ben. Why hadn't she talked with the two of them? Where had they been for the last four days? Then the pianist began playing the bridal march. Anna dismissed her uncertainty and took her first step toward her groom, Joe Jr.

The wedding was perfect! The wedding lunch at the ranch was perfect! Her groom lovingly smiled at her throughout! Joe Jr. leaned over to kiss Anna, and he whispered to Anna, "I guess I've finally done something that pleased my papa." Anna looked at Papa Joe. He wasn't smiling. He was looking straight at Joe Jr. Papa Joe didn't look pleased at all. Anna had noticed throughout The Ranch lunch that Joe Jr. have been drinking more than she had ever seen him drink. As she thought about it, she hadn't ever seen Joe Jr. drink until these last three days. Ever since they had sat down for The Ranch lunch, Joe Jr. had only set his glass down to fill it back up. He had told the waiter to leave the bottle. Every time the bottle was empty, he had asked for another. All these thoughts went through Anna's head after she saw Papa Joe's disapproval. Did Joe Jr. have a drinking problem? Anna had never been around anyone with a drinking problem. Were the wedding activities responsible for Joe Jr.'s drinking problem? Anna felt so guilty.

Papa Joe stood up and announced that the newlyweds needed to change clothes and get going to the airport. Anna had planned on saying thank you to everyone, but Papa Joe rushed them to the room that was designated for them to change clothes. Anna was stunned when Papa Joe came into the room with them. As if Anna was not there, Papa Joe grabbed Joe Jr. by his tuxedo shirt and yelled right in his face.

"You listen to me! You drunk! I am not going to let you ruin this. I'm not going to let you ruin everything! You are drunk, and you are going to sober up even if I have to pour the coffee down your throat myself."

Anna was stunned! She quietly took her clothes and went into the adjoining bathroom. She felt scared for the first time in her life. Anna took her time dressing. She could hear them arguing. She was not going to walk back into that room while they were yelling at each other. She locked the door and waited until it was quiet in the other room.

Anna began to hear what Papa Joe was saying. It sounded like he was saying, "You are not going to ruin this for me. This is my chance to combine our properties, and your drunkenness is not going to get in the way again. All your life I have gotten you out of one mess after another. Now you can't stay sober until *my deal* is complete?"

Anna wondered what deal Papa Joe was talking about. Maybe she had misunderstood. She looked at her watch and realized it was time to leave in order to get through security at the airport. The airport was now hurry up and wait. You had to hurry up to get through security, then wait two hours once you made it through security. Anna wasn't complaining. All her life someone had looked after her safety. She had learned at a young age, she didn't need to know why. If security said jump, she jumped. This was no different. She quietly opened the door of the bathroom and saw Joe Jr. dressed casually. He said, "Let's get moving, my bride." The way he said it was like a two-year-old being made to pick up his toys.

Anna and Joe Jr. left the room hand in hand and ran out the side door. The car was waiting and so were all the guest! A bright smile lit Anna's face. She loved her friends in The Ranch community. It was wonderful to see them all one last time before she left for the airport. Immediately Joe Jr. told the driver, "Ray, we're in a hurry." Anna looked at her watch, a Rolex Papa Joe had given her the night Joe Jr. had proposed. They were within the window of time to get to the airport without any problems. Anna didn't say anything to Joe Jr. about the time because he looked angry, so angry he was shaking. His expression made her scared to even draw attention to herself. She had seen that expression on Wolf's pups, and she knew to stay still and quiet.

During that quiet time, Anna had wondered why their driver wasn't Marion. This was one of The Ranch limousines, and Marion was always her driver. She then remembered that Joe Jr. had called him Ray. Her best guess, Ray was one of Papa Joe's drivers. Then why weren't they in one of Papa Joe's limousines. Anna couldn't dismiss it from her mind. It was just a ride to the airport, but something about it bothered her.

Joe Jr. and Anna had made it through security and were on the way to their gate. The first bar they came by, Joe Jr. said, "I am going to get a drink. I will meet you at the gate." Anna was both hurt and relieved that Joe Jr. had not invited her to join him. Anna found their gate easily.

There was a wedding party already at the gate. The bride had on a veil and a sash that said, "The Bride." The groom had on a top hat and a sash that said, "The Groom." The rest of the wedding party had on sashes identifying their roles. Even the guest had sashes that said, "Guest." Anna had to laugh! They were all having a wonderful time. The bride and groom were inseparable. Thinking that made Anna wonder what was taking Joe Jr. so long. Anna looked around for a quiet spot and found two rows of chairs facing each other behind the check-in desk wall. Anna closed her eyes and went to sleep. Anna had no idea that she was being watched.

Matt had walked around the wall of the podium to call his office and check in on a patient. But he felt his heart stop when he saw the beauty sleeping in a chair behind the wall! Her hair was a golden blond, and he could tell if she had been standing it would have hung past her waist. He decided she was a golden goddess! He thought everything about her was perfect! He wondered what color her eyes would be. He could tell she had no makeup on and her lashes were long and dark. A perfect frame for any color of eyes. Then he noticed those long legs. He was six feet four. He thought she must be at least six feet one. He could not stop staring. He was a professional. In his business he saw many beautiful women. He had never felt like this about any woman before. He tried to analyze what he felt for her. He decided he felt love and protectiveness. Realizing that, he woke out of his trance.

Chapter 2

ANNA WOKE WHEN SHE HEARD their plane being called for boarding. She opened her eyes slowly, and sitting across from her was the most handsome man she had ever seen. His dark hair and dark lashes on that perfectly chiseled face were the icing on the cake. His physic was just as chiseled as his face. How could any man be so perfectly handsome? She could tell by his breathing he was not asleep, he was just resting with his eyes shut. He had to be six feet four at least, and she loved that about him. She had been taller than the boys her age all her life. Even with Joe Jr. she tried only to wear flats since he was her height, six feet one. She came fully awake with the thought of Joe Jr. The handsome man also awoke! They were looking straight at each other. He could see the color of her eyes. They were so blue they were almost violet. Perfect.

Then Joe Jr. came around the podium wall. The stranger noticed the man was drunk, and by his expression he was a mean drunk. Joe Jr. grabbed her arm as if to help her up, but there was a twist to her delicate arm. Anna noticed Matt's eyes turn dark.

Everyone had boarded the plane. Anna put on her seat belt and closed her eyes. Joe Jr. immediately asked for drinks. The male steward told him that he would serve him the minute they were off the ground and the captain has turned on the light that it was safe to move around the cabin. Anna felt Joe Jr. tense, then he pinched her arm. He would not stop. Anna leaned into him and said, "Stop, stop, you're hurting me." Tears were in her eyes, and her arm was bleeding. Anna looked up to see the handsome stranger looking at Joe Jr. with those dark black eyes. She thought, *If looks could kill!* Then she smiled at the handsome stranger, and his face transformed into a smile! Anna looked down and saw the blood on her dress. She stood up got her bag from the overhead compartment and started toward the bathroom nearest the steward area. Joe Jr.'s drinks were being delivered. It was as if he didn't even see her. When Anna reached the steward area, she asked for a first aid kit and the steward pointed to the wall. Before Anna could get the kit down, a baritone voice came from behind her asking to help. She looked up knowing that voice had to belong to the handsome stranger.

He said, "I'm Matt. I'm a plastic surgeon."

She was breathless, and when he looked at her smiling up at him, he was breathless. The steward said they could use that area, it was bigger and private, to bandage her arm. They both laughed because neither was thinking of her cut arm until the steward said to bandage her arm. She finally got her voice back and said her name was Anna and she would be happy to accept his help. Matt moved quickly to set up a sterile area to rest her arm on. He washed his hands at a side sink, then he moved Anna over to the sink and began cleaning the wound. He asked her continually if she was okay. They were standing side by side, and it seemed very natural to both of them. He seemed to have everything he needed in his medical bag. Even though the steward had said they would have more room, it was still a very small area considering their height. They finally figured out the best way to fit in the space was to sit in the two steward chairs that faced each other and for her leg to be between his legs. They both felt the intimacy. He stopped a moment, then continued. He set up another sterile area. Quietly he told her that he had cleaned the wound as best he could with what was available. He would also like to put a few stitches in her arm. He said, "I have lidocaine and will deaden the area. Are you okay?"

It was then when she said for him to do whatever was necessary. He told her it might be better if she talked to get her mind off what he was doing. In his whole career he had never said that to a patient. He knew immediately why he said it. He wanted to know more about her. She began by telling him that she was a veterinarian. She had known from a young age that was what she wanted to be. She told him that as soon as she could walk her dad had bought her a miniature horse. She wasn't even twelve months old. Her mother let her ride Daisy all over the yard, but when her dad came home for lunch, he would let her ride with him to do whatever needed done around The Ranch. Then he would bring her back to the house for a nap. Her dad was always asking her what she wanted now she had Daisy. One day at lunch she heard her mom and dad talking about a cow that was in labor, but it was early and the calf might not survive. (Anna knew if a calf was weak or if something was wrong with it, the mother might reject it). After a minute Anna told her daddy, "I know what I want. I want that baby calf. I know I can make it survive!" There was nothing that could have pleased her dad more! He was laughing and saying, "Yes, yes, yes." And her mommy was crying, "No, no, no, Anna's too young."

After lunch Anna had gone with her daddy to see the mother cow. Anna walked right up to the mother cow and started talking. She was telling the cow that everything was going to be all right, that her dad knew everything and he would take the best care of her. Then she began telling the mother cow that she was going to take her calf and raise him, where someday the calf's mother would be really proud of her calf. Anna's daddy said, "Guess you said the right thing, baby doll. Here comes the calf!" Anna ran around to where the calf was coming. She immediately started talking to the calf, telling the calf she was going to call her Martha and how happy she was that Martha would be given to her! Anna never stopped talking, telling Martha all the adventures they would go on. Then her father said, "Baby doll, you have got to move back. Martha doesn't have the strength to get her legs out." Anna's dad would tell later that Anna said, "Well, Daddy, you should have told me. I'll help her." And Anna put her little arms inside the calf's mother and brought the legs out, and the baby calf slid out on top of Anna. Anna's giggles could be heard throughout the quiet of the barn. All the cowhands had been stunned silent. Anna rolled around with the calf until she could clear her calf's eyes and nose of the gunk and breathe into her baby's nostrils. The calf wobbled onto its feet, and Anna hugged and hugged Martha, all the time talking to her, telling Martha she would meet Daisy tomorrow and they would all be best friends and more! When Anna, her daddy, and Martha got up to The Ranch House, her mother had a bottle ready for Anna to feed Martha. Anna's mommy then told Anna she would show her how to fix the next bottle for Martha.

Anna looked at her arm, and it was all bandaged up. How long Matt had been finished she didn't know. Anna looked at Matt, and this time he had a twinkle in his eye! Anna said, "That's not even the end of this story. The next time my daddy had a cow having a hard birth, he came and got me. I delivered my second calf, Martha II, before I was two years old. Everywhere I went on, Daisy, Martha, and Martha II followed. My mommy came undone and told my daddy that night that I was going to be a girly girl if it killed her.

Matt could not contain himself, he bust out in a belly laugh, and so did Anna! There wasn't any chance of Joe Jr. hearing because the whole wedding party Matt was with had been playing games and celebrating since takeoff. The announcement came to return to their seats. Had she really spent this whole flight with Matt? It had been wonderful!

Matt told Anna to be sure and see a doctor when she got home. He also said he had covered the wound with a waterproof bandage so if she got in the water she needed to take off this outer bandage afterward and check to make sure the waterproof bandage stayed sealed.

Anna and Matt returned to their seats. Joe Jr. had moved to the window seat, so Anna sat down in the aisle seat. Matt was now sitting right across the aisle from her. Matt had just taken the aisle seat when he heard the man with Anna say, "What's with the bandage? You are such a diva." Matt could feel Anna stiffen. Why was she with this man?

Chapter 3

THE PLANE LANDED, AND AS before, Joe Jr. headed into the first bar he saw, telling Anna he would meet her at the luggage bay. As all the wedding party that had been on the plane ran by, Matt walked up to Anna and asked if she was okay. She swayed into Matt, and as she did, Anna put her arm around Matt's waist. Matt put his arm around Anna to support her, and they walked slowly toward the elevator. As the elevator moved to the lower floors, Matt wrapped Anna in his arms and looked in her eyes. Anna wanted to stay in Matt's arms forever. Anna wanted Matt to kiss her. She had never felt a desire like this before for any man, not even Joe Jr. As they got off the elevator, people kept walking by, hurrying to get to their next destination. Matt told Anna he was concerned for her. She admitted she was more than concerned, that in her life she had never had any reason to be afraid, but now she was afraid.

She quickly told Matt that on the way home from her graduation from the school of veterinary science at Texas A & M, her parents were killed in a car accident. Her plans had been to come straight home and work side by side with her dad. She did return home, but it was to take care of all the arrangements for her parents and take care of The Ranch as well. The Ranch had a great foreman and good cowhands, many of whom had been there for years. Her parents left her more than able to take care of The Ranch and others businesses. She told him her daddy had started her helping with the bookkeeping when she was ten and by the time she was thirteen she did all the bookkeeping. As her daddy had invested in other areas of business, she took on each business's records. Anna said all that to say she was aware of every aspect of her parents' businesses. When she came home, Papa Joe, whose fence line joined hers on the north, was the first at her door to offer help. He said his son was finishing up some of his master's coursework but would be home within the next week.

Anna stopped talking. She could tell the luggage was arriving by the noise of the crowd. Matt knew they must hurry.

He said, "I think I know where this story is going."

Anna said, "I never knew Joe Jr. was a drunk, and it has taken me the last four days to recognize it. We live in a close community. Papa Joe was always the spokesperson for Joe Jr., where he was, what wonderful things he was doing. Papa Joe must have paid a lot to keep it quiet."

It was then when they heard Joe Jr. He must have lost his balance because you could tell by the conversation they were helping him.

Matt quickly told Anna that it looked like they would be staying at the same resort. He wrote his cell phone number on the back of a card and handed it to her. He said, "Call me." Then he added, "I'll find you." He walked behind Joe Jr. while she looped behind the elevator and waited by the luggage. Lucky for her, someone had taken her luggage off the carrousel and she was standing by it. A porter asked her if she wanted help, and he had it loaded by the time Joe Jr. spotted her. Joe Jr. didn't address her at the luggage carrousel or as they were walking to the bus.

As Anna stepped on the bus, she saw Matt. She couldn't help but smile! Matt smiled back. Joe Jr. was far enough behind her that he didn't see the exchange. He also didn't see Matt move his medical bag out of the seat across from him and signal Anna to take those seats. Anna had already started to move into the window seat when she heard Joe Jr. yell, "I want the window seat. It's hot as hell in here." Anna visibly stiffened when he started yelling. Then it dawned on her what Joe Jr. had said and she moved into the aisle seat, smiling.

Joe Jr. started complaining before they were even off the airport property. It was too hot! The bus needed new shocks in the rear end. He went on and on. Anna figured most agreed with him but to most it was an adventure on their way to play in the sun. It was the road to Paradise. Anna kept her eyes shut! She was thinking of Matt. She could feel him near. Then she opened her eyes because there was pain shooting up her right arm. Why? That was not the arm that Joe Jr. had pinched. She looked down to see Joe Jr. had her arm with both hands and was digging his nails into her arm. It felt like he was tearing her arm apart.

She said, "Stop, you're hurting me."

Joe Jr. growled, "I need a drink."

Anna said, "I need you to stop hurting me. My arm is bleeding." Anna could feel Matt get up and move beside her. At the same time the bus stopped and a girl with a heavy Jamaican accent jumped on the bus and said, "Welcome to Paradise. I will be your guide."

Joe Jr. could think of nothing but liquor and no one but himself. He pushed past everyone that was also trying to get off the bus and was the first person off. The guide asked him if he would like a cocktail, and he said, "*No*, I want to know where the real liquor is."

The guide looked at the drunk and knew immediately that this must be the guy whose fraternity sent him a gift.

Matt had taken the time to look at Anna's arm. He put three large gauze bandages on it and wrap it in Anna's shirt that she had in her carry-on bag. Anna was losing a lot of blood. He needed to treat her immediately.

As Anna and Matt were getting off the bus, she heard the guide say, "Are you Joe Jr.? You have a gift from your fraternity brothers in your suite. Suite number 7." She handed Joe Jr. a key and pointed the way. The guide looked at the others in the group and handed out keys and said she would be giving them a short tour and then would answer any questions.

Matt put his hand on Anna's back, and they walked up to the desk. Matt introduced himself as a surgeon and asked if they had a medical facility he could use. Anna started shaking. Matt didn't know if it was her pain or her loss of blood. He knew he had to do something quick. The desk clerk saw Anna's arm was bleeding through a blouse that was wrapped around it. Matt was hardly finished speaking before they were escorting them around the side of the desk to a room for medical emergencies. Matt helped Anna get on the bed. She immediately lay down. Matt was asking her if she felt nauseous or faint.

She said, "I just feel pain." Anna could see Matt was furious; but then he stopped, took a deep breath, and looked into her eyes. He could see her pain. She could see his compassion. He told her that if he was doing this procedure in Dallas, he would have used anesthesia and he was truly sorry it was not available.

Anna said, "I trust you."

He started to give her two painkillers he knew were not going to be strong enough. The resort doctor came in and welcomed them while walking straight to a cabinet. He unlocked the cabinet and revealed more controlled drugs than Matt had ever seen in one place. Matt picked two of the drugs he regularly ordered for his patients' pain and picked an IV antibiotic. The resort doctor also said his medical training had been in America. He asked if he could observe or assist. Matt agreed.

Anna closed her eyes, but the pain was not letting up. She could hear both doctors talking but could think of nothing but the pain. Then she was asleep.

The doctors both washed quickly. Then they unwrapped the blouse and revealed the blood- soaked gauze. The doctors started working quickly and efficiently. They seemed to be intuitive about each other's next move. Matt was not pleased. They didn't seem to be able to get the wounds clean enough. The resort doctor suggested leeches. Matt agreed. Matt was looking at the deepest of the ten wounds. Matt was watching the leeches carefully. Then he said, "I think I've found the cause of a lot of her pain." Matt stepped back, and the resort doctor looked at a broken bone in her lower arm.

"We have X-ray," the doctor said. "Not the latest but good enough for us to see how to set this bone."

They rolled Anna into the next room and begin positioning her for best view. Matt was thinking the bone break was lined up, but he took X-rays from every view he could think of to confirm. The resort doctor told Matt he didn't have any plaster to cast but he did have a few plastic forms that would help keep her arm stabilized. He could call an order in for plaster and have it by 10:00 a.m. for casting the next day. Matt agreed and the doctors removed the leeches. Matt immediately started stitching.

The resort doctor was amazed how small and even Matt's stitches were. He couldn't believe Matt could make a half-moon wound into a straight line.

Matt had started stitching at the bottom of the wounds when he got close to where the broken bone was. He stopped and started stitching from the top down. Matt had the resort doctor's headlamp on, and as he was stitching, he was looking for any evidence of debris. He wanted to make sure they never had to go back into these wounds for any reason. Now all that was left to close was the wound where the bone was broken. Matt decided to use Band-Aid stitches because tomorrow the X-ray might show movement and he wanted to set the bone properly. They covered all the wounds with waterproof bandages, then covered again with larger waterproof bandages. Then they covered the whole wound area with gauze. The resort doctor produced a plastic cover that could be tightened to fit Anna's arm.

As the doctors were cleaning up the area, Matt realized that he didn't even know the resort doctor's name. Matt apologized and asked his name. His name was Dr. Jamar. Matt apologized again and thanked Dr. Jamar for opening up his clinic to them, for supplying the medications, for supplying every supply needed to complete the surgery, and, most of all, his skill in treating Anna. Dr. Jamar was excited about the compliments because after working with Matt, Dr. Jamar very much admired the surgeon's skill and technique. Dr. Jamar and Matt finished cleaning up the area. Dr. Jamar said he needed to visit a few patients. Then he stunned Matt by giving him two keys, one to the clinic door and the other to the medicine cabinet's door.

Chapter 4

Matt watched Anna sleeping soundly. The front desk was only two or three steps from the door to the doctor's office. Matt left the door open to make sure Anna was always in his sight. Matt first asked at the desk for the travel agent. Then he asked at the desk for the person in charge of the spa. Matt completed his arrangements and crossed the three steps back to the medical clinic, sat down by Anna's bed, and watched her sleep. He had such strong feelings for her it was hard for him to understand.

Anna woke up, and Matt was looking at her lovingly. Oh, what did she know? Maybe he looked at all his patients like that. But when he said, "Glad you're awake, love," all doubts were erased from her mind.

Matt began telling her all that he and Dr. Jamar had done, except the leeches! He told her they had discovered her arm was broken and what they had put on her arm was just temporary. They would cast it in the morning when the materials arrived. Then Matt picked her up and carried her to the spa. Two ladies were waiting on her. He sat her in a chair and asked for water. They brought back a bottled water. Matt had been asking Anna if she felt any nausea or lightheadedness. She told him no and that she did feel pain but it was much less than before. He handed her the water and a pill for the pain.

"This is not as strong as the others I gave you, but I don't want you to be in pain. If you are feeling pain, contact me. I'm in suite 5. The wedding I'm here to attend is tomorrow at six with a dinner on the beach at seven. Tonight is the rehearsal dinner, which is a cruise, and I'm not required to attend. Bye, love."

She was listening but really not hearing until the "Bye, love."

The spa ladies took her clothes off and lowered her into a bath. The sides of the bath were very low, only about two thirds of her bath at home, but the water covered her. She also realized that the tub was long enough to lie down and stretch her legs. The ladies set towels on the sides and put her arms on them. It made her remember that she wasn't to get her arms wet. They kept saying, "Doctor Matt tell us exactly what to do." Anna realized the top of the tub had a curve dropping down like the shampoo sink at her salon. The ladies put a small pillow and towel in the curve area, then they carefully laid Anna down on it, draping Anna's hair over the top and down the other side. Anna was very comfortable. One lady began by washing Anna's hair, and the other was bathing Anna. It was like a warm, sudsy massage. Anna shut her eyes and enjoyed the luxurious feel of the ladies' hands.

Anna realized that they had finished with her hair and were now using a heater that was gently blowing to dry it. She also realized that there was a continuous circulation of warm water replacing the water, never allowing the water to cool. She decided when she got home she was going to check into getting a tub just like this. Once again Anna closed her eyes. She started dreaming of herself and Matt in this tub. She could envision them lying side by side in this tub. She pictured how beautiful his body would be and how easily they would fit together. Then she opened her eyes slowly because the ladies were asking her if she could stand up so they could dry her. Once again her imagination took her to Matt, and she could feel his tenderness toward her. Was she really thinking this? She had never taken a bath with anyone, not even her mother. She remembered running late for some event when she was just a child and her mother had said, "Just jump in with me." She had told her mother she could get her own bath and be ready before her mother was ready, and she was. She was always independent. Why now was she thinking of her and Matt. She thought immediately of her parents. They were truly two joined as one.

The ladies slipped a beautiful silk shift over her head. It had flowers, the many colors of her eyes. She loved it, the feel of it and the many colors in it. She wished it was hers. She tried to tell the ladies that this wasn't her dress. They said, "Dr. Matt take care of everything." The dress had matching silk shoes. They fit perfectly as well. Matt was so attentive. He had not only arranged this luxury all to meet her needs, he had found a dress complementary to her eyes, her style, and even her pale skin. She had spent her life outdoors, but her mother never once let her go without sunscreen. Anna smiled thinking about her mommy insisting her daddy reapply if they were out for any length of time. He did it too because he wanted Anna with him as much as she could be. He always said he was competing with her girly girl schedule and he wanted all the time he could get. Anna left the spa with a smile on her face. She loved the silky feel of her hair, her skin, the dress, and the shoes. She was Matt's girly girl now.

Chapter 5

ANNA WAS WALKING TOWARD SUITE number 7 when she saw the door to suite number 5 opened and Matt stepped out. She gave him a huge smile and walked right past her suite to Matt's.

"Are you okay?" Matt seemed to always ask that first. It sounded like an endearment to her. Then he said, "You look beautiful, Anna."

"Matt, you are looking very handsome," Anna said quietly. She could hardly breathe.

It was like they had all the time in the world. They stood admiring each other. Nothing needed to be said. They were both very pleased with what they saw in each other.

Anna broke the silence. She said, "If my daddy ever saw me look at a man this way."

Matt said, "Or if he ever saw a man look at you this way."

They both burst out laughing. Anna felt overwhelmed by her feelings for Matt. She loved her parents, but this was love and desire, a very strong desire. She could see Matt felt the same. Anna wanted to breathe in his nostrils where he would follow her everywhere. Anna started to laugh, and watching her laugh, Matt began to laugh.

She said "I was thinking I should blow in your nostrils."

Matt laughed and said, "I will follow you everywhere."

Then they kissed unaware of anyone watching. Unaware of anyone at all.

Anna went into the second door of her suite hoping Joe Jr. had stayed in the adjoining room. She heard him loudly snoring, so she quietly opened the door to the get her luggage. The first thing she saw was a stack of cases of Royal Crown. There must have been a dozen cases. His gift from his fraternity brothers. Joe Jr. turned over and started talking. Anna couldn't understand what he was saying. Anna ran from the room, but Joe Jr. jumped up and barred the door before Anna could get into the adjoining bathroom. Anna's body went slack, and he pushed her aside and said, "Let's go to the beach." Anna was thinking if she went with him she could get out of this room and away from him. She quickly slipped into the first bathing suit in her luggage, picked up her cover-up and her bag, and headed out in front of Joe Jr. He picked up two bottles of Royal Crown and headed out beside her. They crossed a bridge that would have been picturesque under any other circumstances. Anna was only looking for escape. Joe Jr. opened one bottle, then the other, and, holding one in each hand, started taking turns drinking out of each. Anna was praying he would pass out. She didn't know how much you had to drink but surely he was close. She sat down on one of the recliners thinking Joe Jr. would sit. Instead he grabbed her arm, saying, "Let's go for a swim." Anna realized she knew one thing about Joe Jr— he couldn't swim. She had found out in the last four months that he had been courting her that his mother had drowned. He now feared going into deep water. Anna first answered him that she could not get her cast wet. But Joe Jr. had answered her by calling her a diva and telling her it was just plastic. Anna knew she was a strong swimmer. Like everything in her life, her parents made sure she could swim at an early age because The Ranch had acres and acres of water and her parents always thinking ahead to keep her safe.

Joe Jr. wrapped his arms around her from behind and started pushing her toward the water. She scanned the beach and could see two couples suntanning and another looking for shells. They had not even noticed Anna and Joe Jr. No one was in the water. A shiver went up her spine, but she was still thinking she could get away from him by swimming to deeper water. They were in shallow water when Joe Jr.

grabbed her by her hair and dunked her into the water. He let go of her hair in order to strip off his shorts and boxers. Anna got her breath and realized as he ducked her again exactly what he wanted. She might be a virgin, but she knew exactly what he wanted. He slammed her head into his groin area. The water had been stirred up by Joe Jr.'s stripping. Anna could hardly see, but she was looking for a way to pull him into deeper water. She thought, *I'm going to drown right here, right in this awkward position.* Then Joe Jr. stepped back, and as the water was stirred up again, Anna saw a lobster coming up right behind Joe Jr. When he went to get his balance, he stepped back again and the lobster pinched his butt and held. Joe Jr. pulled Anna up by her hair and yelled, "Stop pinching me!" Anna was catching her breath, showing Joe Jr. that her hands were free. When he yelled again and started running out of the water onto the beach, Anna dived. She swam into clearer water before she came up for breath.

Chapter 6

WHEN SHE STARTED WALKING OUT of the water, the beach was empty. She would learn later that Joe Jr. ran screaming to the suite while the lobster hung on. The vacationers that saw him and those that could hear him started running after him with their cell phones clicking. It turned into an airport panic! Like when a couple of people run to change gates, then a few more, then everyone is running to check the flight board or change gates. Everyone was trying to get the best picture. Anna looked up, and the only person on the beach was coming toward her. She knew immediately it was Matt. He stopped, but she didn't know why. Then when she got close enough to see his eyes, she knew. Desired! She hadn't realized the suit she had put on. Her total focus was on a way to escape when she had picked up the suit.

Matt breathlessly said, "My golden goddess." She had on a one-piece shiny gold swimsuit, and with her golden hair and pale skin, the sun made her look golden. That was not all. Matt noticed that the suit was nearly translucent when wet. Matt knew then he could never get enough of his golden goddess! He picked her up and carried her to the emergency clinic to check and bandage her wounds.

Anna lay on the bed in the emergency room. Matt didn't tell her that she didn't need to lie down for him to bandage her arms. He took his time to enjoy the view. When Matt heard Dr. Jamal coming, Matt pulled a sheet over Anna's body. But the image was burned into his brain. Matt began removing Anna's bandages. She was very fortunate that none of the waterproof bandages had leaked. Matt cleaned her arms and bandaged with fresh bandages and a new plastic cast.

While Matt was busy with Anna, people kept coming to the emergency treatment room door and telling the "lobster boy" wanted a doctor. Dr. Jamal kept saying, "We are in surgery. We will be there as soon as the surgery is complete." The people would turn and walk off laughing.

Matt could tell Anna was tired. Her eyes were getting dark underneath. He carried her to the adjoining room of her suite. He gave her another dose of pain medicine. She fell right to sleep. Anna's purse was brought to the suite by an attendant. Matt had to walk through to the adjoining room to answer. Matt took the purse and cover-up from the attendant. As he started back to Anna, he saw her luggage. He picked that up as well and placed it in the room with Anna. He saw Joe Jr. passed out on the bed. No lobster. Matt checked the two doors adjoining the suite and bathroom, making sure they were locked. Then he lay down by Anna.

They were awakened by yelling. They could hear Joe Jr. yelling but not at Anna. He was yelling at Papa Joe. Anna went into the bathroom that adjoined both rooms. Matt ran in after her.

Matt said, "Don't listen to him. He is just talking trash."

But Anna responded, "No, Matt, he is talking about my ranch."

They were both paralyzed to the spot, listening.

Joe Jr. was talking to his father about marrying Anna. He said, "You want me to stay sober to marry that bitch. Don't tell me what I can say. You've called her a bitch since her birth. Why don't you just kill her, then you can have The Ranch and everything you've wanted and I can go back to drinking to forget how you killed my mother for her ranch. You think I didn't know all the things you've done just to get your hands on my mother's ranch and now you're going after another. Dad, did you kill Anna's parents? Why do I ask? I know you killed them. You think I'm a disgrace, but I'm not a murderer."

Matt looked at Anna, both knew that something was wrong with this conversation. Matt opened the adjoining door that was furthest away from Joe Jr.'s voice. He signaled Anna to join him. Joe Jr. was in the room alone. His body language was as if he was arguing with someone in the room. He was not on a phone. He was not on a speaker. He was not on a Bluetooth. He may have been reliving a conversation with Papa Joe or maybe this was the conversation Joe Jr. wanted with Papa Joe. Then Joe Jr. passed out and fell to the floor.

Matt shut and locked the door, then went to the adjoining bath and unlocked the door. He stepped across the bathroom and locked the bathroom door leading to the room that Joe Jr. was in. He stepped back into the room where Anna was and locked that door. Anna's room was as secure as he could make it. He appealed to her to please just stay with him. Anna felt she had the complete picture of what Papa Joe and Joe Jr. we're trying to achieve. Papa Joe was using Joe Jr. by having him stay sober and marry Anna.

Chapter 7

IF ONLY ANNA HAD MET Matt earlier, she would have known what it was like to love and desire to be with a man. She knew the love of her parents, and she still loved them. It was the desire for a man and the desire to share every aspect of her life with him that she had never known.

Matt was pressured by the groom's dad into going on the rehearsal dinner cruise. Matt had rescued the groom's dad from bankrupting his legal practice. The attorney had showed Matt his appreciation many times, but he would be offended if Matt turned down the invitation. Matt wanted to stay with Anna, but she assured him she was locked up safe. Plus she had some calls to make to The Ranch. Matt left, and Anna felt alone as soon as he shut the door. Anna took out her cell phone and called Marion. Anna had hoped he and Ben would be together where she could talk to them both. Marion and Ben had been a part of her life since she could remember. They were both around her parents' age and had seen her grow up on The Ranch. Anyone that saw them together could see the love they had for her.

Marion and Ben had both been foremen and lead ranch hand for her daddy. Then as she had gotten older, Marion and Ben had started driving her everywhere. She knew her daddy considered them her bodyguards. She considered them friends.

Anna told them everything that had happened to her in the last twelve hours. She included the conversation between Joe Jr. and Papa

Joe while they were changing clothes. She told everything, including Joe Jr.'s drunken conversation with himself. Anna was crying, and Marion and Ben were crying.

Anna finally asked, "Did Papa Joe kill Mommy and Daddy?"

They were always honest with Anna. They began telling their story. The reason they had missed the festivities leading to the wedding was because for the first time some people had actually come forward with information about her parents' car wreck. They had been too scared before to come forward, but now they weren't afraid. They had lived in fear of Papa Joe long enough. Papa Joe knew they had information that would convict him. They had kept quiet to protect the only son they had left after that fatal wreck that killed Anna's parents. Their only son left had colon cancer and died last week. Papa Joe was paying for their son's treatment. When he died, they contacted Marion and Ben and they had several clandestine meetings. They have given them all the information they needed to prosecute Papa Joe. They weren't able to get the documents until the day after her wedding.

"We are so sorry we couldn't stop the wedding. We were trying to convince ourselves you were not marrying Papa Joe, you were marrying Joe Jr. If we had only known he was a drunk… We never even suspected until we heard what several people were saying the day of the wedding. We are so sorry, baby girl!"

All three were crying so hard no one could talk. Anna got her voice back first. She told Marion and Ben that now they knew what Papa Joe had done and what his plans were, they needed a plan. She told them her plan. They questioned some aspects, and the three agreed on the plan. Anna concluded the call by saying, "I'll be home tomorrow. I love you, Ben! I love you, Marion!"

They both replied, "We love you, baby girl!"

Next, Anna called her ranch foreman, but before she could say hello, Doug started in. Papa Joe had moved five hundred head to her bottomland. According to the foreman he had been too late to stop him. The only thing he could think was, there was a traitor among his ranch hands that had revealed their guard's gate rotation. He told her about the new house Papa Joe was building on the back 120 acres. Doug had tried to put a stop to the construction, but Papa Joe knew a lot of the construction contractors, and he had promised to double their invoices if completed by Saturday. He had named several contractors in the area, and neither Anna nor the foreman wanted to see them go unpaid. Lastly, he said that The Ranch bull was being moved back to The Ranch today. He felt Papa Joe knew it and was putting his cattle with their cattle for them to get bred.

Anna told the foreman to surround himself with a dozen trusted ranch hands. He was to send the other ranch hands to work on the fences on the riverbed. He should also send a cook with them where they could stay in the riverbed bunkhouse. He and his trusted men were to move Papa Joe's cattle to the loading pens at gate 8. He was to allow the house on her property to be finished. The Ranch bull was to be moved in for breeding their herd after Papa Joe's cows were penned. Then she said, "I'll be home tomorrow. Don't tell anyone. If you need me, call me. There's no honeymoon going on here!"

Then Anna called the family attorney, Jason, and told him what papers she needed. She told Jason to have the papers typed up by the most confidential legal secretary he had. He told her he could still type. She asked him to fax her copies. She said, "Marion would pick up the originals." She also wanted her attorney to set up an appointment in two days for her to meet with the district attorney. She wanted the district attorney and not an assistant. She wanted the meeting at the attorney's office and kept under wraps as much as possible. She told her attorney that Marion and Ben would also be present. Then she said, "Marion, Ben, and I can keep a secret. Can you, not your office, but you? I also want assurance from the DA that he doesn't leak that we are meeting. If you need me, call me. Bye, Jason, you're the best."

Jason was laughing when he hung up. He had been Anna's escort to many events starting when they were three years old. Her mommy always chose him for her because he was taller than her and he could dance. They continued going out to any event that required escorts. It pleased their mommies. Anna was always loyal. She attended every basketball game he played from junior high through high school, at home or away. Even his parents didn't make them all. After every game she always said the same thing, "Jason, you're the best!" After high school graduation, Anna went to Texas A & M while Jason's scholarship took him to the University of Oklahoma. He married an OU cheerleader and had two children. He had moved home to open his own law practice. When the ranch attorney passed away, Anna's parents gave all the ranch work to Jason and his practice thrived.

Anna had finished all her calls when there was a knock on the door. She was scared to answer. She finally asked who it was, and it was the photographer. She had totally forgotten the photographer she had hired for her honeymoon. She had no idea if the photographer had gotten any photos.

Chapter 8

Anna opened the door. The photographer was carrying a box of photos and a large handbag. Anna asked her in, and they sat at a table that could seat eight. She started showing photos to Anna, beginning with Joe Jr. stepping off the bus. Wow, it was so obvious to Anna now that he was drunk. Then Anna and Matt was getting off the bus. Her arm was wrapped in a blouse. The other arm was bandaged already. Then Anna lying still on the hospital bed and Matt was leaning over, talking low to her. She even had a picture of the damage before the doctors had started cleaning her wound. The whole surgery was recorded on print.

"When you called before you arrived, you said take pictures of every moment."

Anna looked at her and said, "You did an excellent job. You have truly captured my trip." Anna told her she wanted her to continue. Anna wanted two five-by-sevens of all the shots and two five-by-sevens of every picture she took from here on. She told the photographer that she was leaving tomorrow, but Joe Jr. would be here until Saturday. Anna asked her if she could mail one set of prints to Anna's PO Box, a place no one but Anna could retrieve them. Anna said she would stop by the photo shop before she boarded the bus for the airport and get any other photos that were ready. Anna gave her $10,000.

The photographer said, "This is way too much for what you're asking."

Anna said, "You have done exactly what I asked. This was not the honeymoon I thought it would be, but I have to say your pictures are worth a thousand words! You have lived through this trip step by step with me, and you have viewed things no one could have expected. Consider this combat pay."

As the photographer was leaving, she said, "See you tonight."

Anna had forgotten all about the dinner on the beach tonight. She had purchased a gold dress just for the evening. She was going, and she would enjoy, thanking the lobster that had come to her aid.

Anna had noticed during the visit that her arm was hurting again. After the photographer left, Anna took one of the pills Matt had left with her. She took off the beautiful flowered silk and packed it. She only had her carry-on in her room with the gold dress in the closet. She had meant to pack it last but had forgotten to put it in her check-in luggage. Matt had a porter move her luggage to the emergency medical room where Anna could have them when they boarded the bus going to the airport. Matt didn't want Anna to have any reason to return to her room after he got back from the rehearsal dinner cruise. Matt was hoping Anna would stay with him.

Anna lay down to sleep in her slip. She fell asleep dreaming of the gold dress. Anna woke up with a start. What had woken her up? Then she realized Joe Jr. must have busted the door from his room to the bathroom. She was so groggy she couldn't seem to react. She wanted to get up and leave, but she couldn't seem to keep her eyes open. Then Joe Jr. burst through the door to her room.

He was yelling, "I've got a message for Papa Joe." Then he hit Anna in the face with his fist. He said, "Give Papa Joe this message." And hit Anna again. She passed out and was unaware that Joe Jr kept repeating, "This is for Papa Joe," and hitting Anna until he passed out on top of her.

The photographer saw that the candlelight dinner was ready and the server was there waiting for Anna. Fear gripped her. She ran to Anna's suite. She knew Anna always left the outer door unlocked. Had Joe Jr. figured it out? Had he gotten in her room? She burst through the door, and Joe Jr. was lying on top of Anna. Anna had blood all over her face.

Anna spoke, and the photographer jumped. "I thought you were dead."

Anna said, "I'm going to close my eyes, and you take all the pictures that you think captures what he did to me. Don't forget the busted doors."

The photographer got to work, and Anna fell back to sleep. Anna woke up when she felt the photographer trying to move Joe Jr. off her. Together the two of them were able to roll him off Anna.

Anna got two bottles of water and poured them over her face. She was using makeup pads to clean the blood off her face. She brushed her hair and slipped the gold dress over her head. The photographer couldn't believe the change. A few minutes ago Anna looked dead. Now she was one of the most beautiful women in the world. You could easily see the cuts on her face, but the total package made you forget them.

Anna walked down the stairs to the beach. This was the first time the photographer had given Anna any direction. The golden girl at sunset. Anna's movements were beautiful. The photographer wondered what kind of training Anna had. She could easily be a model. The waiter appeared to be caught up in the movements of Anna. He had never seen any woman as beautiful.

Anna sat at the table surrounded by a heart drawn in the sand. She asked the waiter for bottled water. She told him she would be dining alone. He served her soup. After she had taken a few bites, he noticed she took a pill. He assumed it was because of her arm. She remembered what she had ordered previously and knew she had no appetite. She asked if she could have the lobster course next. He left to get the lobster course. It was then that Anna said, "I'm sorry, I don't even know your name."

The photographer responded, "My name is Allison."

Anna told Allison that she wanted to give the lobster a send-off of thanks. "I want to thank her for saving me!" Allison caught on quickly. The waiter arrived with the lobster, and Allison started directing Anna.

The waiter caught on as well. They all ended up sending the lobster to paradise.

Anna told the waiter all she needed was a couple of bottled waters and the check. He did exactly what she asked. She added 25 percent to the check and signed. When she handed him back the receipt, Anna said, "I know we were told not to tip you, so I'm giving you this gift for your wife."

The waiter looked at the photographer, and she had her back turned, taking picture of the dinner cruise coming into port. He slip the cash between two of the buttons on his shirt and said, "My wife thank you for the gift."

Anna looked at the cruise. She was looking for Matt. She longed for him, for his kiss, for his touch. The injuries to her face had vanished from her mind. She could only think of Matt. She was sure they would be together for the future.

Matt borrowed the captain's binoculars. Matt saw Anna sitting on the shore. She was safe! This had been a miserable dinner for him. He could hardly eat anything. He was sick with worry and mad at himself for coming on this dinner cruise.

Anna stopped watching the water and turned her chair where she could see the bridge and path Matt would take to the beach to her.

As Matt approached, he could see her sitting in the candlelight. He thought, *She is beautiful. She is mine.*

Anna stood and started toward him. He could see she was dressed in a gold dress that clung to her figure. She was his golden goddess! He said a silent prayer to her mommy.

"Thanks, Mommy, for my GG. She was your girly girl. Now she is my golden goddess. Thanks, Mommy."

They rushed to meet each other. They hugged and kissed and kissed. Anna didn't want him to ever let go of her. She felt safe, and she wanted more. She asked him what he was smiling about when he was watching her approach.

He said, "I was talking with your mommy. I was thanking her for her GG, girly girl. I told her she did wonderful. She could be proud. You are now my GG, golden goddess."

They were both laughing when the moonlight caught Anna's face, and Matt saw the new wounds.

"I'm so sorry, Anna. I should have stayed with you. Please forgive me."

They were both crying as they walked to the emergency medical room.

Matt said, "From now on I'm going to be just as protective as your daddy was."

Anna tried to reason with Matt. It was not his fault. She felt safe locked in the room. It was her fault that he was able to get to her. Then Anna replied, "No, I'm not taking the fault for what happened and you're not either." Anna continued by telling Matt that the only one at fault was Joe Jr.

Chapter 9

THE DOOR TO THE MEDICAL exam room was already opened, and there was a girl about Anna's age. She told them immediately that she was Dr. Jamar's nurse and she knew the history of Anna. Matt picked Anna up and laid her on the examination table. While he was talking low to Anna, the nurse opened the cabinet that held the drugs. She showed Matt an antibiotic IV bag, a saline IV bag, and a smaller bag of narcotics. Matt smiled and asked her name.

She replied, "My name is Nurse Jamar. Dr. Jamar and I are married."

Anna and Matt gave her huge smiles.

While Nurse Jamar attached the IV bags and put an IV port in Anna's arm, Matt found the magnifying glasses in his bag. He also put on Dr. Jamal's headlamp. He wanted as much light as he could get. He washed his hands and put on gloves. Nurse Jamar followed his lead and washed and put her gloves on. Yes, Nurse Jamar knew this patient. She and her husband had talked at length about Anna and Dr. Matt. They were very concerned for her and thought Anna and Dr. Matt showed feelings for each other.

The other issue that Dr. and Nurse Jamal had discussed in the evenings was whether to tell Nurse Jamal's older brother about Joe Jr. Her brother was on the police force and was head over the region. She looked at Anna's face and made her decision. She would call her brother the minute she finished assisting Dr. Matt. Dr. Jamal had told her that Anna and Dr. Matt were leaving tomorrow, but Joe Jr. would be here through the week. She had heard through the resort staff that he had totaled the suite. That was enough cause for her brother to visit Joe Jr.

Dr. Matt's every move was precise and efficient. Dr. Jamal had told her that Dr. Matt was a plastic surgeon in the US. The nurse knew he cared for Anna and this surgery was in his field of study. Anna was in the best of care. Nurse Jamal watched Anna's vitals and her breathing. She kept her eye on what Matt was doing as well. She watched him make each cut on Anna's face disappear. It was amazing! The surgery went well of course. Dr. Jamal would have said, "The surgery went as expected." When Matt was finished with Anna's surgery, he started cleaning the surgical area. Nurse Jamal stopped him, signaling him to monitor Anna. She would clean the area. The room was quiet after Nurse Jamal finished. She had left quietly.

Matt never left Ann's side. His world was right there on the surgical bed. He knew he loved Anna. He knew he never wanted to be apart from her. He knew how her daddy had felt.

The first thing Anna saw when she opened her eyes was Matt. He was crying.

She said, "Don't cry, love."

Matt began smiling through the tears. "Anna, my Anna, love. I love you now and forever."

Anna responded, "I love you forever, my love." Anna closed her eyes and slept.

Matt's laughing woke Anna up. He told her he was thinking she may not remember what she had said. She told him that she would never forget. Forever was forever.

Matt began telling Anna that they were pretty much the talk of the resort. He had found out while on the cruise that the staff and guests were waiting for him to take her away from that drunk. He said he had checked up on the flight after he had stitched her second arm.

"We are booked on the first flight, but it is not until tomorrow." Then he realized it was 1:00 a.m. and he said, "Today." He had checked on places at or close to the airport, but there was nothing available. He asked her to please consider staying with him. He was in a suite, so there would be plenty of room.

She wanted to know about the wedding he was here to attend. He said the wedding is at 11:00 a.m. with a luncheon afterwards. He told her that they would all understand if he is not able to attend. He offered for Anna to go with him to the wedding, but she felt safer staying inside. She was very adamant that he should go. Joe Jr. had not come out of the suite since the lobster pinching him. She felt she would be safe in Matt's suite.

They quietly talked another hour, then locked the medical room and walked hand in hand to Matt's suite. Matt insisted they stay in the room that had two queen-size beds. His desire for Anna was strong, but he put her into the bed farthest from the door, and he took the bed by the door. It had nothing to do with Joe Jr. It was all about Anna. He wanted Anna to be safe. He wanted her to be able to rest after the traumas she had been through. He loved Anna. Anything he could think to do for her, he wanted to do.

Anna woke up around 9:00 a.m. Matt was at the door letting a porter in with breakfast. It smelled wonderful, and the resort's display of the breakfast was five star. Anna and Matt sat and enjoyed the luxurious feast. They discussed Anna's ranch and Matt's surgical practice. The things they learned about each other made them love and admire each other even more.

Matt started getting ready for the wedding. Anna took the fax she received and started looking over each one carefully. She also went through the pictures she already had and chose several.

Matt was ready to leave, and Anna said she would like to go to the spa and have a bath. Matt called and made the arrangements. They walked out of the suite together, and he kissed her good-bye at the spa. The ladies were the same ladies that had taken care of her both times. They kept repeating, "Dr. Matt tell us what to do." Anna could tell they were carefully looking her over. She knew her body had many bruises that were starting to show besides the new stitches on her face. Anna knew the routine now, and it comforted her. She stepped in the bath, and the ladies began. The bath was luxurious! She knew they were finished with her hair because she could hear the soft purr of the heater. Once again Anna felt silky. There was no other word. The ladies finished drying her and slipped a silk dress over her. She was amazed at the feel of the silk. It was so light, and it was a beautiful cream color. She loved it. The two ladies escorted her out the door, and two large men in tan uniform stepped in behind them.

They were all nearing the top of the stairs when something happened that Ana would only find out later. She was only aware that Joe Jr. came out his door and took her to the ground, then the pain to her breast was so intense she passed out.

Chapter 10

The story around the resort was that "that drunk" came out his door and pushed Anna to the concrete second floor walkway and stared eating her flesh, her breast. The two ladies tried to stop him, and he pushed one over the second floor rail to fall ten feet to the ground. At the same time the two men pushed past the second spa lady as she ran down the stairs to check the other lady. The two men kicked and beat on "the drunk," but he would not release Anna's breast. As they picked him up, they were hitting his jaw multiple times. He finally let go, leaving behind three teeth in Anna's breast. The uniformed men took "the drunk" no one was sure where, except Nurse Jamar. She saw her two brothers take Joe Jr. behind the building and load him in their Jeep and drive away.

The wedding was dismissing when they heard the commotion. Matt ran toward the noise, realizing that it was coming from the building where his suite was. There were people around a girl underneath the stairs. Matt breathe a sigh of relief when the people started saying, "She's alive. She's alive." But when he caught a glimpse of the girl, it wasn't Anna. He ran up the stairs and saw Anna bleeding. There was so much blood. Matt picked her up and ran for the medical emergency room. As he cleaned Anna, he could not stop crying. He had left Anna at the spa with the two guards Nurse Jamar recommended. What had gone so wrong? He collected himself and realized most of the blood was coming from her breast area. What had Joe Jr. done to her? Had he knifed her? Then he saw the teeth marks and the three teeth. He thought he would faint.

Dr. Jamar came in with the wounded girl and asked if Matt was okay and could Matt handle the surgery alone. He needed to tend to the girl. Matt nodded his head in agreement. He completed cleaning Anna and made all the preparations for the surgery.

Anna opened her eyes, and Matt quietly told her that he was not able to use an IV pain medicine because he needed a second person and the Jamars were busy. He gave her two pain pills, and she went to sleep. Matt was meticulous with his surgery. He was unaware of anyone but his Anna. When he was finished, he picked up Anna and took her to the spa. Nurse Jamar said that the lady who had fallen had no broken bones. Her breath had been knocked out of her, and she had a slight concussion. She offered to help Matt bathe Anna. Everything was set up, and Nurse Jamar helped Matt lower Anna into the warm water. Nurse Jamar started washing Anna's hair, and Matt started washing her body.

Anna opened her eyes and said, "I dreamed of this. I dreamed of you and I bathing."

Matt gave Anna a huge smile and handed her another pain pill.

While Anna was asleep, they continued to bathe her. Matt was seeing a lot of bruises on Anna that were not visible before. Matt curled up in a fetal position and began to cry. The nurse walked over to him and laid her hand on his back. She talked to him quietly, telling him that the two guards with Anna were her brothers. They were both policemen. In the past, when there were similar incidents, the police, led by her brother, would come in and take the troublemaker. She said it was common that the person was drunk. After years of experience, the police would hold the person in a drunk tank. The police would keep Joe Jr. in the drunk tank until it is time to put him on the plane with his ticket to return back home.

She also said she had already given her brother Joe Jr.'s plane ticket. She went on to say that there was only one entrance or exit from the drunk tank. Joe Jr. will not be able to escape. He will receive bread and water three times a day until he can keep it down! Then he will receive bread and milk and water. He will have one shower a day with sixty pounds of pressure. That is enough pressure to clean up after him. He will be dressed from his luggage. Before he boards the bus to the airport, they will hand him over to the marshal on the plane. He will be handcuffed until the plane lands.

She went on to say that the resort had Joe Jr.'s American Express and that the renovations that were needed because of his actions, plus the medical bills for the spa lady, had already been approved. She said all the bills from the shops are coming in now and they will be paid by Joe Jr.'s American Express.

Matt's smile returned to his face as they lifted Anna and started drying her. He put a violet silk shift over her head and once again with matching shoes. Matt whispered in her ear, "You are so silky! Your hair is silky, your skin is silky, and your shift is silky. I love every silky inch of you."

They walked out of the spa and were amazed! The wedding party was lined up on each side of the sidewalk, cheering. After them the staff had lined up to join the cheering. Anna only had eyes for Matt as the cheering went on and on until their bus pulled out of the parking lot. Anna's mouth was dry, and she looked in her carry-on bag for a bottled water. It was there. She saw a large envelope and opened it. In it were all the pictures and a note that said, "More to come!"

Chapter 11

WHEN THEY GOT OFF THE bus at the airport, there were four men in uniform waiting to escort them. Two of the men took their luggage to check-in and brought the tickets to them. The other two escorted them through security, through the waiting area, and out to the plane. They told Anna to board, and then the tallest of the men told Matt that the next six days Joe Jr. would be in the drunk tank sobering up. Then he described the drunk tank.

"The drunk will get bread and water three times a day. The drunk tank is washed out once a day with a water pressure of sixty pounds. This will also be considered his daily shower. He will not be able to escape because the only opening is from the top. He will not come out of the hole until the day we take him to the airport."

Matt didn't interrupt him even though Nurse Jamar had already explained it to him. Anna hadn't gone to her seat. She had heard everything from the door. She came back out and hugged both men and thanked them for saving her life.

Matt and Anna boarded the plane together. Anna told Matt she could hardly keep her eyes open. He told her to close her eyes, she was safe.

When the flight started announcing that they were cleared for landing, Anna woke up. She told Matt that they needed to talk. She said she imagined Papa Joe would be at the airport at her gate.

Matt said, "He will have to have a ticket to be at the gate."

She said, "Whatever it takes he'll be there." She told Matt that she needed him to walk down the ramp but to stay a few feet behind her. "I have something to say to Papa Joe that I want you to hear." She asked him to sit in an area near enough to hear them, then to just take his ticket out like he was making a connection or act like he's was on his cell phone listening to messages.

He wanted to know if she was strong enough to do this. She laughed and told him no one had ever asked her that question. Then she asked him to stay near, that would give her strength. If he stepped forward, that would make her look weak to Papa Joe and Papa Joe would pounce on her.

Matt did as Anna instructed. When they got close to the end of the ramp, she dropped Matt's hand. He saw Anna evolve. As he came down the ramp behind her, he heard someone say, "Here's my Frankenstein daughter."

Matt glared at the old man, but before he could come to her defense, he heard Anna say, "No, Frankenstein's bride."

"Now, darling, you don't look that bad, just a couple of scratches. No cause to play the drama daughter."

Anna reached in her bag and brought up what looked like legal papers and pictures. She handed Papa Joe the first paper and said, "This marriage will be annulled. When Joe Jr. gets home Sunday night, you need to bring him to The Ranch's attorney's office Monday morning at nine and for him to sign this paper in front of a notary and two witnesses."

Papa Joe puffed up like a toad and yelled, "On what grounds, little daughter."

Anna continued, "The grounds for annulment are on the paper. The marriage was not consummated."

"You mean to tell me you're a virgin at twenty-two years old. I'll believe that when hell freezes over," Papa Joe yelled.

Anna said, "I'll have the proof from two medical doctors by Monday at nine that I am a virgin. Now the second document doesn't involve Joe Jr. You, Papa Joe, can take care of it immediately. You are to get your five hundred head off *my* ranch. You don't think I would know what was going on at my own ranch. You have tried to get that herd on my bottomland twice already, and I want them off tonight."

Papa Joe sputtered and whined, "Well, baby daughter, you know I can't round them up and get them off by tonight. Why, it would take me most of the week."

Anna said, "Your herd has been separated and are in the corrals at gate 8. Bring your trucks and get them loaded and off my property."

"Well now, hold on, little missy. What about your bull?"

Anna answered, "What about my bull?"

Papa Joe said, "I know you brought him home. He probably got with my cows."

Anna replied, "No, but that was your plan, wasn't it? I charge half a million dollars for my bull to breed. You think I'm going to let him get with your scrawny breed? I had my bull transferred and penned 'cause I knew that was what you were up to." Then Anna continued, "Now let's talk about this third document. Once again you don't need Joe Jr to get this taken care of. You are going to sign this paper, giving me the new house plus all its contents that you built on my property without my permission."

"Why you little drama queen! I'll do no such thing. Who do you think is big enough to make me?"

Anna calmly reached into her bag and brought out pictures of each of her injuries. She showed Papa Joe the pictures while saying, "The law is going to make you, that's who. The ranch attorney already has a court date for next Wednesday. So if you don't take care of these little things by Monday at 9:00 a.m., I'll see you in court on Wednesday. Also, if I hear you went to the press, I'll publish all these photos and more. You listen, Papa Joe, I will publish all the photos and more." Then Anna handed Papa Joes the photo of her breast.

Papa Joe headed for the restroom. Maybe the photo upset him, but he was probably calling his attorney.

The tall cowboy with Papa Joe stepped up to Anna and said, "You did great, girl. Your daddy would be proud of you."

Anna said, "I wish Marion had got to hear me."

Ben tapped his cowboy hat and said, "He heard and saw it all. He kept celebrating in my ear. It's a good thing I'm half deaf."

Then Anna said, "I have a gift for you." She got out a beautiful sack and pulled out a jewelry box. She opened it where he could see. It was a necklace with a rugged gold nugget in the shape of a heart glittering with diamonds. She put it around his neck, then turned it over so he could read it. Tears were in his eyes when he said, "I love you too, Anna." Then he turned to Matt and said, "Is that the surgeon?"

Anna said yes and threw Matt a kiss. Ben handed Anna a packet. Then Papa Joe came out of the bathroom.

Anna handed the packet to Papa Joe and said, "This is a copy of all the documents. Plus another that will be served when Joe Jr.'s plane lands. It is a restraining order. He is not to be within fifty feet of me."

Papa Joe said, "I'll load up and move the cattle this afternoon. I just wanted our ranches to be joined."

"Our ranches will never do business," Anna said. "Joe Jr. is never to step on my ranch!"

Papa Joe said, "What are you going to do, shoot him?"

Anna answered, "I'll send my wolf pups to eat his flesh. No one would ever find him."

Papa Joe turned and left.

Ben smiled and tipped his hat at Anna and followed Joe Sr.

As soon as they were out of sight, Anna and Matt were in each other's arms. He told her how strong she was and how he loved her.

She said, "Well, that was The Ranch owner you just saw."

He said, "I've just fallen for The Ranch owner."

They went to the luggage carousel, and their luggage wasn't there, but they could see Marion standing by the limousine waving at them. Marion told them as they walk out that their luggage was loaded. Then he and Anna were in a big bear hug. Anna got out another beautiful sack and reached inside and brought out a jewelry box. She opened it where Marion could see what it was. It was a nugget of gold ring shaped like a heart covered with diamonds. She turned the ring where Marion could see the inscription inside. He read it and said, "I love you, Anna."

Anna put the ring on his finger, and he said, "You the surgeon?" to Matt.

They all got in the car, and Marion never stopped talking until they turned into the front gate. Then he turned to Matt and said, "I guess you're staying for supper."

Chapter 12

MATT HAVE NEVER BEEN ON a ranch. He was amazed at the size of The Ranch operation just from what he could see. Anna's ranch had beautiful fencing made of stone. The fence went on for twelve and a half miles. He knew by the mile intersections. Then they went under the stone entrance. It was so tall and wide that two stock trucks could go through it at once. It was also secured by an automatic gate and a caller box for guest. Matt noticed the elaborate landscaping from the gate to the house. He looked at Anna, and they both said, "Mommy." They were both laughing when they stopped at the house. Anna said, "Welcome to The Ranch House."

The house must have had three stories, and all three stories were made of stone. The stone that the fence was made of was beautiful. There were stone columns, and it crossed Matt's mind that this must have all come from the same quarry. Inside the home, every room was huge. Anna asked Matt if he wanted to meet the wolf pups. Matt asked if she would protect him. The entryway had two staircases coming down from each side, reminding Matt of a horseshoe. They went through the dining room, and the table was already set for six. It was set with fine china and crystal. Matt was pretty sure the silverware was sterling silver! Then they went into a kitchen that had professional stoves, ovens, and refrigerators that had see-through doors. The kitchen was three, maybe four, massive kitchens as one.

At one sink stood a lady in a red dress. Anna introduced her as Jewel. Jewel gave Anna a huge hug, then she gave Matt a huge hug. Nothing was said, but they all ended up with tears in their eyes.

Anna said, "I've got a gift for you." And once again she pulled out a beautiful sack, then took out a jewelry box. Then she opened the box where Jewel could see the gift. It was a beautiful ruby stone necklace and ruby earrings. Matt had seen that set in the resort jewelry store window. He knew it was quite valuable. Matt looked at Jewel. She was beaming! She looked about the same age as Anna's parent would have been.

Jewel said, "Now where am I going to wear this?"

Anna said, "Everywhere and every day."

Jewel said, "Okay, you're the boss! Now go on and see the pups. They have been crying the whole time you were gone. I tried to tell them you would be back. I even fixed them steak, but they wouldn't eat. Ya'll go on now, and I'll bring you some supper to feed them."

They went through several more rooms that were maybe a pantry or a mud room. Well, Matt couldn't put names to them, but there were four. Out the back door was a porch that went from one side of the house to another. Matt thought it probably went around the whole house. There were several sets of lawn furniture and flowers in colorful pots. Anna took Matt's hand and told him to just sit quietly on the steps. He would know when he was welcomed to the group.

Wolf came out first. She was coal black. Anna lay down on the grass at the bottom of the steps. Wolf went right to her. It sounded to Matt like Wolf was crying. Matt watched as Wolf went first to Anna's left arm. Anna started talking to Wolf. Matt could hear most of what she was saying. It sounded like she was telling Wolf she was okay. She was glad to be home. She was glad to see Wolf. Wolf licked her hand and smelled the bandage. Anna said, "Joe Jr."

Wolf growled, baring his teeth. Matt had never seen anything as ferocious. Anna kept talking as Wolf moved around her. Wolf looked closely at her face and made the crying noise again. It seemed Anna was telling Wolf that she was okay. He once again thought he heard Anna say "Joe Jr." At that Wolf bared her teeth and growled. Anna did not seem to be in the least bit frightened. Wolf went next to Anna's broken right arm. Anna was talking low, but Matt thought she was saying that she was getting better. She would be okay. Then once again Matt could tell by Wolf's reaction that she must have said the name of Joe Jr. Wolf leaned his head close to Anna's breast. Wolf cried and howled. Anna was crying! Matt was crying! Wolf lay down gently across Anna. Wolf was just under Anna's breast.

Matt quietly walked down the steps and lay down on Anna's other side. Anna took Matt's hand but continued talking to Wolf. She was talking so low that Matt couldn't hear what she was saying. Then Wolf stood up and put her paws over Matt and lay down across both Anna and Matt. Wolf had stopped crying, and Matt started imitating Anna's movements. She was stroking Wolf slow and deep in her fur. Wolf licked Matt's face, and there was a gasp from behind the screen door.

Matt and Anna could see the three faces watching them. They were all crying. Matt and Anna were not aware, but there were two more faces watching them. Anna's heads of security were also watching the monitors and crying. They had seen Anna's wolf many times, and Wolf ran with them, seeming to realize they protected Anna. But Wolf had never taken anyone into the friendship Wolf had with Anna.

Wolf lifted her head and turned and saw her cubs waiting to see Anna. She stood up carefully, stepped across both Anna and Matt, and went to the cubs. Anna started getting up, and Matt followed her to the porch steps. He realized immediately why when the pups in all sizes came out to greet them. Wolf took a stance of protectiveness right by Anna. If the wolf cubs got too lively, Wolf would make a slight sound and they would sit up immediately. The wolf pups were playful with Matt as well. He continued to follow Anna's lead. Then the two smallest pups lay down in Matt's lap and curled up in balls of fluff and went to sleep. The larger wolf pups lay on the ground at Anna's feet. It was as if they knew Anna was injured.

Matt wasn't aware of time, the pleasure of sharing this aspect of Anna's life was overwhelming. Then the screen door opened, and Jewel said she had the wolf pups' supper. She went on to say that Wolf had not eaten since Anna had left. Jewel said, "You've been home and back your whole college years. I've never seen Wolf crying and refusing to eat." Jewel put Wolf's plate down first. It looked like several steaks. Then all the wolf pups lined up by size with the last two having what looked like ground beef and milk. Even seeing them line up to eat was amazing to Matt.

Jewel said, "You two need to come in and wash up for supper."

Anna and Matt got up and went into a side room by the door they had gone out. It was a bathroom, and it looked like five good-sized men could wash up at the same time. Anna and Matt remained quiet while they washed their hands and faces. Matt washed Anna's face gently and helped her wash and dry her hands. It was very intimate.

Jewel told them to go on into the dining room. She would serve the meal as soon as Doug got here. He was on his way. There were six places set at the table. Marion and Ben were standing by two of the side chairs. Anna stood by an end chair. Matt was at a loss. He finally asked where he was to sit. Marion said, "Right here's where you belong," pointing to the other end chair. Anna looked at Marion and Ben. She knew this was a milestone. Marion was giving his chair to Matt. Before anything could be said, they heard Doug, Anna's foreman, come in the back door and go to the washroom. In a few minutes he came into the dining room, helping Jewel carry the dishes of food to the table. He made several trips to the kitchen. It looked like they were going to have a feast with all of Jewel's favorite recipes on the table.

On one trip to the kitchen, he nodded at the dining room and said, "New seating arrangements?"

Jewel nodded an uh-huh.

When Doug and Jewel sat down, Anna asked Matt if he would say a prayer. Matt had so many things he was thankful for, he began immediately. When he finished, five happy faces were smiling at him.

There was no lack of conversation at the table with Ben, Marion, and Jewel catching Doug up on what had been happening since Anna's plane landed, including Wolf and the pups welcoming Matt into their circle. Doug could hardly believe it. What he had learned tonight explained the new seating arrangements.

Doug reported on what was going on at The Ranch. Doug told Anna who the two traitors had been. No one at the table was surprised. Doug had sent a couple of ranch hands from his trusted circle to the riverbed bunkhouse plus security had concealed cameras with sound, and it didn't take long to confirm their suspicions. Payday was going to be Friday, and Anna told Doug she wanted to be there. Doug made his good-byes, saying he needed to get back. There were still things to do that night.

As Doug was getting up, Anna directed him, with everyone following, to the closest bedroom. Matt thought this bedroom could possibly be for Doug when he stayed in The Ranch House. Doug just looked like he belonged in it. Doug looked at the new saddle on the bed and jumped on it like it was his long-lost woman. He hugged the saddle and rolled all over the huge bed. When he stopped, he looked straight at Anna. Doug said, "Better than a woman, but don't go telling Belle. Thank you, Anna. How'd you know?"

She said, "As soon as I saw it, I knew it was meant to be yours."

Doug left The Ranch House with a big smile on his face.

Chapter 13

Jewel started clearing the dishes, and Anna started to help. Matt gently put his hand on her back and said, "Not this time. You all should hear this." They sat back down at the table. Matt explained that Anna needed to take it easy tonight and possibly longer, depending on what the doctors will tell Anna tomorrow. "Anna, you have a broken arm. You've had a concussion, and you have been under anesthesia, plus your other injuries all in the last few days. Tomorrow morning I have arranged for you to be seen by a neurologist. He is in sports medicine and works with the Dallas Cowboys. He has an excellent reputation, plus has seen a lot of concussions. He will be able to do an MRI on you right at his facility. He will also talk to you about your concussion and what precautions you will need to take."

Anna had tears in her eyes when she kissed Matt on his cheek.

Matt continued, "After we see him, we are going to see an orthopedic doctor in the same complex. He will be setting your arm and casting your arm."

Anna hugged and kissed Matt, telling him, "Thank you," again and again.

Jewel, Ben, and Marion could see the love.

Anna told Matt that she had also made appointments with two gynecologist to prove she was a virgin.

Jewel said, "I'm thinking one is your gynecologist you have been seeing all your life. I hope the other is Dr. Jessie Banks."

Anna nodded her head yes.

Jewel turned to Matt and continued, "Dr. Jessie Banks had a daughter the same age as Anna. Her daughter, Allison, was killed when a drunk driver hit a group of children in the school crosswalk. She was only nine years old. Anna made a book of stories and pictures of Allison for Dr. Jessie. Dr. Jessie has never forgotten. Anna still visits her and adds to the book if she hears any new stories or finds other pictures with Allison."

Jewel gave a sly grin and said she had it on good authority that Dr. Jessie had a long relationship with Judge Barker, actually back to when they both lost their spouses.

Marion and Ben both burst out laughing, saying in unison, "Jewel, where do you hear this stuff?"

Jewel said, "I never reveal my source."

Jewel then headed toward the kitchen with both hands full of dishes. Matt followed her with both his hands full of dishes. Ben, Marion, and Anna followed closely. Jewel started washing and putting up leftovers while Matt dried the dishes. Matt opened a few cabinets and drawers that were handy, and he was able to put everything away but three large bowls. The conversation never stopped. They were laughing, crying, and making plans on how to shut down Joe Sr. The dishes were done, and there was a break in the conversation.

Marion said he had already placed Anna and Matt's luggage upstairs. He said, "I placed you in the room right next door to Anna's. It's only separated by a bathroom." Then he surprised everyone by telling Matt that the room he was staying in had two massive beds and it might be better for Anna to stay with him in case she needed anything in the night. Everyone laughed, and he turned red and said, "I don't mean that. Why, the girl has a concussion. Don't you dare take advantage of her."

Anna said, "Well, I might take advantage of him."

They all went to bed feeling happier than they had been since the news that Anna's parents were killed.

Matt gave Anna a couple of pain relievers. She went fast asleep. He lay on her bed for several minutes watching her, then got in the other bed. He was fast asleep. Then he heard Anna whimpering during the night. He lay down with her and started talking quietly. Her breathing settled, and she had never woken up that night. He went to sleep lying beside her.

Matt woke up early. He was used to early surgeries. He took a shower and dressed, then woke Anna. He talked softly to her, telling her he loved her and how beautiful she was while he helped her bath. He helped dry her hair and body. The bruises were even more prominent than before. Then he said, "By any chance do you have a silk blouse that opens in the front and pants with no metal. I'm thinking about all your appointments and how you need to dress."

Anna chose a three-piece silk outfit. It was an oversized shell with an oversized silk jacket and silk pants. It was violet.

Matt said, "Beautiful," while helping her slip it over her head.

They headed down to the dining room. The table was set for two, and the sideboard was loaded with enough food to feed the ranch hands. They both ate too much and started laughing at their empty plates, wondering where the food had gone. Jewel walked in with another red dress on plus the ruby necklace and earrings. Matt told her she looked very beautiful this morning. Jewel glowed while telling them that Marion had the car out front and was ready when they were. Matt stood up and helped Anna out of her chair, then picked up their plates, heading for the kitchen. Jewel stopped Matt, telling him she had plenty of help in the kitchen. She then introduced Matt to Doug's wife, Belle. She was pregnant with their third child and was hoping for another boy. She loved her boys. This was a perfect place for them to grow up. She was thankful to Anna for introducing her to Doug.

Marion greeted Anna and Matt as he was opening the door for them. Once in the limousine, Anna laid her head on Matt's shoulders and slept. Marion's talking didn't seem to bother her. Once again Marion talked the whole way. He told Matt about The Ranch, about the community, and Anna. Matt hung on to every word.

Chapter 14

They arrived at the Sports Medical Center and were greeted at the door by the neurologist nurse. She escorted them to his examination room and had Anna take off her jacket and blouse with Matt's help and put on the gown. The nurse came back in and took her to the MRI machine. Matt was told he could wait in the exam room if he wanted and that the MRI would take about twenty minutes.

Matt checked his e-mail, and over three hundred pictures had been sent to him. One of the wedding party had organized everyone in the wedding party to send the pictures to her and she would organize and send them to Matt. They all took a pledge to not share any of the photos online or in any way. Most deleted them after sending them to her.

The nurse saw Anna's cast now that Anna's jacket was off and asked Anna if the cast had any metal. Anna explained it was temporary and there were no screws or any other metal. She was placed in the MRI machine and lay comfortably while the nurse prepared her. Anna chose to listen to local news on the headphones that were blocking out most of the MRI machine noise. She knew that by now Papa Joe had a plan. She just wished she knew what it was.

The pictures brought Matt back to a very emotional state. From everything he knew, Anna had between five to seven blows to her head by a man weighing over two hundred pounds. Then added to that Joe Jr. had taken her down on the solid concrete walkway. He was very worried about her concussion or multiple concussions. He then had a glimmer of hope because he hadn't felt any lumps on Anna's head when he had washed her hair. She also didn't have any raised hematoma on her face that might have signaled intracranial bleeding. He was crying and praying when he heard the nurse and Anna coming back toward the room. Thank God his mother had taught him to carry a handkerchief in his front pocket for anyone that needed one and a handkerchief in his back pocket for himself.

Anna came in, and the nurse went to get the doctor. Anna hugged Matt. She could tell he was upset. She started talking to him quietly. She was telling him that whatever the report she could and would follow the doctor's instructions. She would come through this. Matt corrected her telling her they would both follow the doctor's directions and they would both come through this together.

The doctor came into the room. He looked Matt's age. It turned out they had been roommates in college and part of medical school until they declared their specialties. The doctor told them both that "This is probably the best-case scenario for the injuries Anna had sustained. She does have a concussion, but if you played football, this concussion would not take you out of the game. You probably wouldn't realize you had sustained a concussion. Matt told me he hadn't observed you showing any evidence of a concussion. That sounds in line with what I saw. My nurse is going to give you a few timed test before you leave. Then she will make two appointments for you to come back. One appointment in one week, and she will give you the test again. She will also give you a second appointment for you come back again the week after. The second week you return, we will repeat the MRI and test and I will talk to you again. In these next two weeks I want you to relax and give your brain time to heal. I don't want you to drive, that jars your body more than you know. I don't want you riding your horses or any four-wheel vehicles. When deciding what activities you can do, just keep in mind nothing that would bounce you around and certainly nothing that there was a risk to getting your head hit. Do you have any questions?"

They thanked the doctor, and he brought his nurse back in. The nurse directed Matt to the waiting room, and after a short time Anna was returned to the waiting room.

The nurse said, "I understand you also have an appointment with Dr. Reynolds. I will walk you over to his office."

In Dr. Reynolds' office, the doctor's nurse met Anna at the desk and took Anna and Matt back to a patient's room. Anna was instructed to take off her shirt and jacket and put on the gown. Matt helped Anna, then he gave her a pain reliever. Dr. Reynolds came in, and once again it was old home week for the two doctors. The only difference was Dr. Reynolds was a suite mate of Matt's through medical school. Anna really enjoyed meeting Matt's friends and learning more about him. He said the room they were in was set up with everything he was going to need so Anna could try to relax. She was in the best hands in the state. Dr. Reynolds nurse was in the room with them, and she had been getting out the tools, and Anna noticed several syringes. Dr. Reynolds explained that Anna would not be under anesthesia but he would be numbing the area pretty good. He took the plastic cuff off Anna's arm, then the bandages, then the layers of waterproof bandages. He looked at Matt and said, "Preparing to scuba dive. Oh wait, I know the Dr. Matt way—do everything you know to do every time."

Anna could tell Matt was enjoying the ribbing and suspected he could give as good as take. Anna shut her eyes, then reopened, and said, "If you use leeches again, wake me up. I want to watch."

Dr. Reynolds said, "I love this woman!"

Matt knew now that the leeches were out of the bag. He would be ribbed the rest of his life.

The last thing Anna was aware of was the nurse moving the portable X-ray machine over to her arm. She really didn't even know what had been done. She just looked down and saw a gold cast. She began laughing, and both doctors looked at her.

Dr. Reynolds said, "No leeches this time. Matt has all your instructions. Bring Matt back anytime."

They walked out hand in hand. Marion had the limousine right out the front door. He saw Anna's cast and began laughing and talking. When they got into the limo, they saw their lunch was set out for them. Somewhere in all Marion's talking he said something about getting Anna her favorite sandwich from the deli and since he didn't know Matt's favorite he got him the same. Ham and cheese, nothing fancy. Marion did stop talking long enough to hear about Anna's doctor appointments. When Marion continued, Anna whispered, "I like your friends."

Both the gynecologist were in the same medical complex. Matt was glad about that because Anna looked very tired. They went into the office of the gynecologist her mom had brought her since the age of fifteen. Dr. Young had made Anna feel comfortable since Anna's first visit. Dr. Young had given Anna much advice about being joined with a man. Dr. Young had confided in Anna just two months ago that she was also a virgin when she got married. She had been involved in getting her medical degree and licensing just as Anna was involved getting her veterinarian degree and licensing. Anna took it as a compliment that she could identify with Dr. Young and that Dr. Young had confided in her.

Matt stayed in the waiting room. Anna had said the nurse would help her dress. Matt called Jewel. Ben was with her, so they put him on speakerphone. Matt reported about both appointments this morning and how tired Anna was. He asked Jewel if Anna could just have a light supper in her room. Jewel agreed, that it was exactly what her baby girl needed.

When the nurse came out in the waiting room, Anna had a file in her hand. Matt assumed that it was the notarized document. The nurse gave them directions to Dr. Jesse's office. It was just a short distance, but Anna was getting very dark under her eyes. Matt softly asked Anna if she wanted to reschedule. She gently shook her head no, and they continued on. Allison's mother looked just the same as Anna remembered.

Dr. Jesse took Anna into her examination room and said, "My love, I'm not going to put you under any more torture. This will be a quick exam, and I will confirm Dr. Young's report. It will be witnessed and notarized right here in my office." Dr. Jesse did just that.

Dr. Jesse walked back into the examining room with the papers, and she handed them to Anna. Dr. Jesse said, "This Joe Jr. and his papa are going to be put down and put down hard. I can assure you."

Anna said, "I think of Allison often. Here are some more memories and pictures."

Dr. Jesse had tears in her eyes as she walked Anna to the door.

Matt jumped up when he saw Anna. He practically carried her to the car. Marion didn't say a word on the way home. Matt was talking low to Anna. Marion thought Matt was apologizing for bringing her out today. He was saying that she was to have a long healing nap and let her trusted circle surround her and take care of her. He gave Anna two pain relievers, and she went right to sleep. Matt carried Anna up to the room they had stayed in last night. Anna's bed was turned down. Matt took her silk jacket off, arranged pillows for her arms to rest on, and covered her with a light comforter. He turned; and Ben, Jewel, and Marion were standing in the doorway. It was a warm day, probably in the eighties, but Matt asked if the fireplace could be turned on. He wanted her kept warm, but he didn't want to put heavy blankets on her arm or breast. Ben went right over and built a fire. Matt lay down beside Anna and went to sleep while three pairs of eyes watched.

Chapter 15

WHEN MATT WOKE UP, HE checked on Anna. She was sleeping soundly. He could hear Wolf crying. He walked down the stairs and straight out the door. He sat down in the same place where he and Anna had lain down with Wolf the day before. He curled up into a fetal position and sobbed out loud. Wolf went to him and lay as close as she could get to his back. After a while Matt relaxed and turned to face Wolf. She licked the tears from his face. He finally began talking to Wolf, softly confessing how worried he was about Anna. How afraid today had been a setback for her because they had gone from one appointment to another. He had been so anxious about her injuries that he may have done her harm.

Wolf watched intently as if she knew everything Matt was telling her. Finally, Matt fell asleep while Wolf watched over him. He learned later that Wolf had sat watching over him for three hours. When Matt woke up, he went up and checked on Anna, then took a long bath in Anna's tub. He remembered she had wanted a tub like the spa. He got out and dressed. Then he went to his luggage and got all the products he had purchased from the spa and set them in her bathroom. He opened his e-mail, but this time he knew he was too vulnerable to open any pictures. He went to the website the lady at the spa had given him and ordered two bathtubs, one that would easily hold Anna and another that would hold both him and Anna. He remembered that was Anna's fantasy.

He noticed Jewel had brought him some potato soup. It was hot and delicious. He lay down beside Anna and slept. Anna and Matt slept until noon. They awoke slowly, examining each other's faces. Matt was glad to see the dark that had been under Anna's eyes was gone. She looked refreshed. Matt and Anna went downstairs in their clothes from the day before. Everyone was in the dining room. The two end chairs were left open with place settings in front of them. Matt pulled out Anna's chair and helped her sit down. The meal was pot roast, mashed potatoes, and every kind of garden vegetable. Matt knew the gardens hadn't come in yet this year, so his thought was that someone must have canned these. They were delicious.

Marion started the conversation by saying he had taken the notarized papers from both doctors to The Ranch attorney. He also reported that the judge had signed the restraining order against Joe. Jr. and it would be served the minute he stepped off the plane. Then Doug said that Papa Joe's cattle were off the ranch, but security had reported something else. They had learned from monitoring their young traitors that Joe Jr. had plans to make a run on Papa Joe. He had planned before he left for the resort with one of the foremen to start selling Papa Joe's cattle at a sale barn a couple of counties to the north. Doug was suggesting that they keep the young traitors on and keep them closely monitored. That would also mean Anna didn't need to make the trip to the bunkhouse for payday. Matt liked that. Doug continued saying that they were even aware of when and where. Security has already set up cameras. They will even monitor the sale.

Everyone at the table knew that the next sale that Joe Jr. could make would be the Saturday after he got home. That would be after Monday's meeting in The Ranch attorney's office and after the Wednesday court date, but they needed to be proactive with Papa Joe because The Ranch would be the first accused of cattle rustling.

Anna asked what Matt wanted to do today, and all eyes went to him. He asked if it was possible for him to meet the security and see their operation. Anna took Matt up to the third floor. When they stepped on the third floor landing, two men walked up to meet them. They introduced themselves as Cody and Tony. They were massive! They opened each door on the third landing and told Matt what each room was used for. They both had private bedrooms and baths. They had a gym with the latest equipment that took up what had once been two bedrooms. That explained their size. Then they opened the door and announced that this room was security central. It was also two rooms that had been renovated into one large room. There was a private bed and bath adjoining security central. They told Matt that they did a lot of their work at night.

"We like to stay out of sight. Even the ranch hands are unaware of the security. What's secure about it if everyone knows? The people in this house and Doug and Belle are the only ones that know the extent of what we do. We were both in the Special Services and a part of the Secret Service. When we got out of the military, we joined up with the Texas Rangers. Anna opens her ranch to the Texas Rangers for training exercises. That's when we became aware of The Ranch and went to Anna with a proposal. She hired us, and our ranch story began."

Matt wanted to know if anyone monitored the screens when they went out at nights.

Cody said, "We do!" Then he picked up a black backpack and opened it, showing several laptops and iPads.

Matt was very impressed with their professionalism, their knowledge of both the security/surveillance, their technical savvy, and their knowledge of The Ranch. He expressed his pleasure in meeting them and complimented them on their knowledge. Before he turned to leave he said, "Thank you for watching over Anna."

The next couple of days Anna and Matt spent on The Ranch. They were indulged by the members of the household. The primary reason was for Anna to heal. Matt wanted to take Anna to his practice, but his staff was not expected to return to work until Monday. Matt had given them generous bonuses, and they were vacationing. Matt had done this before, and it had worked well in the past. When he took time off, the office closed and any emergencies were directed to another plastic surgeon's practice in the same complex.

The Ranch was aware of Joe Jr.'s plane's arrival. There was a tension in the house. When Matt learned that Cord was at the medical complex because of an emergency, Matt decided to take Anna in for a second opinion on the work Matt had done on Anna's breast. Matt knew the stitches he had done on Anna's face and arms were perfect. There was no infection. He could foresee a great outcome.

Cord was happy to get to meet Anna. She was as beautiful as Cord had been told. Matt and Cord were friends with many friends in common, so Cord had heard about Anna's vicious attacker. Cord admired the work Matt had done on Anna's face. He wasn't able to see either arm, but he knew Matt was an excellent surgeon. Cord and Matt had handled trauma surgeries before together. When Cord saw the pictures of the bites to Anna's breast, he felt nauseous. He had seen dog bites but never human bites. The bites had the appearance of someone trying to eat her breast. Matt had pictures from every angle. He had not been aware that the photographer was even in the room with him and Anna. He realized now though how valuable these pictures are to the medical treatment course that the surgeon would take. Cord took the bandages off Anna's breast and was pleasantly surprised. He pointed to one particular area and asked how Matt had kept the skin from puckering. Matt said he had learned that stitch from Dr. Jamal's nurse.

Cord said, "You teach me that stitch, and we will call this surgery even."

They looked closely at Anna's breast and added four stitches in new areas. They were meticulous. They had taken over two hours. Anna had just had some pain medication, nothing to put her to sleep. Matt didn't want her to have anesthesia because of the concussion. Matt and Cord were very pleased with the outcome. They felt Anna would be too.

Chapter 16

Aɴɴᴀ ᴀɴᴅ Mᴀᴛᴛ ʟᴇꜰᴛ ᴛʜᴇ complex, and Marion drove them straight to The Ranch. Jewel, in another red dress and with her rubies on, had prepared a salad and sandwich bar in the security room. The circle of Anna's trusted friends were waiting for Joe Jr. to arrive. Papa Joe had not noticed the people around. There was a couple and two men that could be seen on the monitors.

Cody said, "See that man sleeping. He has three cameras on with sound."

Matt was really impressed. He knew there was surveillance, but he would never have pick out who. In all, Tony told them, there were thirty cameras. He said they would watch the screens live, then he and Cody would use a software they had written and sold on the condition that the military could use the software at no cost. This software would combine the images of the thirty cameras into a panoramic view with synchronized sound.

The first pictures they started to see were Joe Jr. being escorted off the plane. The marshal took his hands and leg cuffs off. Joe Jr. started down the ramp to the public waiting area. Papa Joe stood up to meet him as soon as the people started coming off the ramp. Joe Jr. was last.

Papa Joe saw him and asked, "That bride of yours beat you up?"

Joe Jr. said, "Dad, shut up. Hell no, I got this in the drunk tank. Every day, when men got off work, they would come by the drunk tank and throw stones at me. They were not allowed to throw any stone bigger than their fists. They would throw and yell, 'Get a job, drunk.' As far as I could tell, it lasted a half hour." He went on talking, saying, "The first day or two I thought the walls were falling in on me. No one watching felt one bit of concern."

Papa Joe started blustering. "We will shut that resort down and that town."

Joe Jr. said, "Dad, shut up." Joe Jr. started walking toward the luggage carousel.

As Papa Joe caught up with him, Matt thought it sounded like Papa Joe was outlining a plan to fight all the papers Anna's attorney had filed. Matt noticed the expression on Anna's face and picked her up and carried her to a seat with a view of the monitors. He sat down and held Anna in his lap. With most of the screens active at one time or another, trying to connect the conversation was difficult. Matt took Anna to their room, and they rested. Jason was coming over at five, and Cody and Tony would have the security disc run through the program they had invented.

Anna and Matt went to sleep and didn't wake until six thirty. It was a consensus of the group to let them sleep. Anna woke first and lay still and watched Matt. She couldn't remember ever thinking a man was handsome. She loved Matt and desired Matt. Now she knew she had found what had been missing in her life, the love and desire Dr. Jesse had talked to her about. Matt woke, and they looked at each other with no accountability of time. They got up and headed downstairs.

Jason took control of the conversation. He told them that with the information he had gotten from security, he knew exactly what direction to counter. Jason went over a few details and told everyone good night.

As Anna was walking him to the door, she said, "Jason, you're the best."

Jason left with a big grin on his face.

Papa Joe had Ben driving again for him. He didn't realize that using Anna's Ben was biting his nose off to spite his face. He just thought he was screwing Anna since Ben was on her payroll. He never dreamed anyone would have the nerve to make a move against him. The circle around Anna had decided that Ben needed to continue driving as long as they were getting information. The same theory as keeping the two traitor ranch hands on.

Jewel must not have slept at all during the night. She had a feast ready when everyone got to the table. None talked much or ate much, not even Marion. Ben and Doug left first with Marion, Anna and Matt leaving a few minutes later. Marion drove, still remaining quiet. When Marion reached The Ranch attorney's office, he parked right in front of the door behind Judge Barker's limousine. There wasn't any room left for any other vehicles. Ben would have to park in the lot, and that would make Papa Joe furious. He was the most important person in his own mind.

Anna looked very composed in a violet suit with sleeves that flared making room for her cast, and Matt was in a dark suit with a violet tie. They were a stunning couple even today appearing before Judge Barker. Matt opened the door, and Jason was there to greet them. Jason took them into a conference room where Judge Barker sat at the head of the table. Judge Barker's court reporter was seated to the judge's left. Jason sat to the right of the judge and directed Anna to sit beside him with Matt on the other side of Anna.

They could all hear Papa Joes yelling over the parking when he arrived. His attorney sat beside the court reporter, then Papa Joe, dressed in his pompous ranch attire, and Joe Jr., dressed in T-shirt and shorts.

Judge Barker's bailiff called the room to order. Judge Barker announced that this proceeding fell under family court and his rulings would be binding. He continued, saying the first petition before the court was the annulment of the marriage between Anna Violet Johnson and Joe Berry Mercer Jr. Judge Barker presented the documents from both doctors and practically dared Joe Jr. not to accept and sign.

Joe Jr. picked up the pen and moved to sign the documents, but before he could sign, Papa Joe Sr. said, "Let's just don't get in a hurry now!"

Chapter 17

JUDGE BARKER GLARED AT PAPA Joe and called him out of order. The judge continued to say that Joe Berry Mercer Sr. had no standing in this decision.

Joe Jr. signed the annulment. No one knew if he was signing it because he felt in agreement or if he was signing it because he knew his dad didn't want him to sign. After Joe Jr. signed the annulment, it was signed by Anna; Judge Barker; and the court reporter, who was also a notary. The two attorneys signed as witnesses.

After they had completed signing, the judge said that the order would be filed today. A roar went up in The Ranch security central where Jewel, Belle, Doug, Cody, and Tony were watching on the surveillance monitor.

Next the judge said there was a bit of housekeeping that needed to be taken care of. Jason handed Joe Jr. and Joe Sr. each restraining orders. He told both men that their attorney could explain the orders.

The judge told Joe Berry Mercer Jr. that he was dismissed as he was not a defendant in the other petitions.

Joe Jr. said, "I would like to let the court know that I have paid for the medical services Anna received and all other charges from the resort."

Joe Sr. said, "I contested those charges."

Joe Jr. never even looked at his dad. He continued saying that he had notified the American Express that the question of the contested charge had been resolved and they have all been paid. He continued by saying that any further medical bills that would be submitted he wanted to be placed on his American Express Card.

The judge signaled the court clerk, and she brought Joe Jr. the papers to sign. She took his credit card and got all the information, and she explained to Anna how and where to submit the bills. After the papers had been signed, Judge Barker told Joe Jr. a second time that he was dismissed. Joe Jr. got up and left. Joe Sr. was left with his mouth open, gaping.

"The other bit of housekeeping," the judge said, "has to do with the cease and desist order against you, Joe Berry Mercer Sr. The order states that on three different occasions you have tried to bring as many as five hundred cattle onto Miss Anna's property, The Ranch, without her permission."

Joe Sr. had been quietly brewing and jumped out of his chair, bellowing at Anna that he had removed the cattle and that order needed to be torn up. Judge Barker told Joe Sr.'s attorney to keep his client under control. This was the judge's second warning and the next time he is out of order he would be removed from this proceeding. Judge Barker then asked Anna what the price would be if she rented her bottomlands. Anna told the judge that in the past she had a minimum contract of 4 weeks and for 500 cattle she would charge $28 a day times 28 days times 500 cattle, which would be $409,248, but those figures were from 4 years ago. "We don't rent out the bottomland because our own herd has grown and we use the land."

Then Joe Sr. started to jump up but caught himself. He just glared at Anna and said, "I don't have no contract with you, and the three times I moved my cattle, they were never on The Ranch for a month."

The judge just let Joe Sr. continue, and Joe Sr. was on a roll, saying, "And one of those times your foreman, you, and those wolves of yours stopped us from crossing the fence line."

Judge Barker said, "Joe Sr., you are to address this court not Ms. Anna. You have brought up the matter of the fence."

Jason had prepared Anna on what to answer if this came up.

Judge Barker looked at Anna and asked what the cost of the repair to the fence was. Anna reported accurately what the fence cost by the foot, how many poles were replaced, how many ranch hands were paid overtime since the incident was at night and the fences had to be repaired immediately, plus the cost of renting generator-powered lights. The total was $29,500. Then the judge looked at Joe Sr. and asked what was the issue about The Ranch bull.

He looked hatefully at Anna and said, "I won't be paying any fees for her bull. She removed my cattle to pens before she let her bull free."

The judge asked, "Were you wanting to get the bull with your cows?"

Joe Sr. said, "Hell, yes, she has the best bull in the state. Why has she got to be so selfish?"

Judge Barker had heard what he needed to hear. Joe Sr. intended to use The Ranch bull to breed his cattle. The judge asked Anna the cost of breeding five hundred cattle with the ranch bull, and Anna responded, "It is $500,000."

Judge Barker said, "I'm ready to rule on the cease and desist order. Mr. Joe Berry Mercer the court orders you to pay Ms. Anna Violet Johnson the sum of $1,500,000 in restitution for the three times you tried to bring your cattle on her property plus your putting your cattle on The Ranch for the purpose of breeding with The Ranch bull."

Joe Sr. got up to leave.

Judge Barker said, "Sit right back down. This court is still in session. Now the last petition is concerning the house you built on Anna's ranch without her knowledge or her permission. Joe Berry Mercer, do have anything to say about this?"

Anna now had a clear picture of Joe Sr. He was a bullheaded man, and it appeared that he had ramrodded his way through most of his life with people being paid to achieve for him anything he wanted. One way or another he seemed to always get his way. So far today the decisions of the court hadn't favored him, and now he was huffing and puffing like a bull in a bull-fighting arena.

Joe Sr. began saying that the marriage between Anna and Joe Jr. had joined the two ranches and he didn't see any reason to have to wait a week before combining the two operations. Building the house was just one aspect of that.

The judge looked with amazement at Joe Sr. and asked, "Who was the house built for? Who did you plan to move into the house?"

Then Joe Sr. answered, "Why, me!" Then as if in a fog, he seemed to forget who he was addressing. His expression changed, and he began speaking.

"I had dreamed of this marriage since Anna's parents were killed in the car wreck. I knew if Joe Jr. could stay sober long enough Anna would be persuaded to marry him, thus joining our ranches. I would then be the owner of the largest ranch in the state, with the best bull in the state. If only Joe Jr. could have played his role, that's where I would be right now instead of bowing down to a woman!"

Joe Sr. was so delusional that those watching were stunned silent.

Judge Barker broke the silence. "The marriage of your son and Anna, even if it was not now annulled, would not have joined the ranches as you have been stating. Your attorney can explain the law to you. I'm now ready to make a judgment concerning the house and the contents in the house that Joe Berry Mercer Sr. built on the ranch without permission. The judgment of this court is that the house and contents belong to the owner of The Ranch, Ms. Anna Violet Carter. It is further ordered that Mr. Joe Berry Mercer Sr. is responsible for paying the contractors and their invoices that were turned in before his deadline. That each invoice would be paid double as promised by Joe Berry Mercer." Judge Barker signaled the court clerk, and she brought the invoices forward, gave a sum of $2,500,000, doubled being $5,000,000. Judge Barker required that all settlements be paid before 5:00 p.m.

Judge Barker dismissed the proceedings and walked out of the room. As he walked out four Texas Rangers and the district attorney walked in. The district attorney read Joe Sr. his Miranda Rights while the Texas Rangers put handcuffs on his hands and shackles on his feet. The district attorney then announced that the charge was two counts of murder of Patricia Violet Carter and Samson Creed Carter. Joe Berry Mercer Sr. was taken and booked in the county jail.

Chapter 18

IT WAS TOLD LATER THAT he had called Joe Jr. and that Joe Jr. hung up on him. Joe Jr. also didn't have to rustle the cattle like he had previously planned when the engagement was announced. Joe Sr. had been so focused on getting Anna's ranch he had given Joe Jr. a power of attorney that if for any reason Joe Sr. was not available to make everyday decisions, Joe Jr. had his power of attorney to make the decisions. He had his ranch foreman take them to the county sale barn the next week. Joe Jr. then took the profits from the sale of the cattle and paid his ranch hands and let them go. It was also enough to pay his own American Express since his dad had not yet been able to access his funds. Because of Joe Jr., his dad was still in the county jail.

Joe Jr. finally went to visit his dad behind bars. It was reported by those working in the jail that day that Joe Sr. immediately started giving orders to Joe Jr. Joe Jr. told him to "Shut up." Joe Jr. continued by telling his dad that he had paid all Joe Sr.'s fines concerning Anna's ranch and the petitions Judge Barker had ruled upon. He notified his dad that his dad's ranch attorney would not be representing Joe Sr. because he was not a criminal attorney. Joe Jr. had paid the attorney bills and dissolved the retainer agreement. Then Joe Jr. said, "Last night I burned our ranch house! I have signed our ranch property over to Anna. I never want to see you again. You are on your own now." Then Joe Jr. walked out of the county jail. He got in a new Chevy truck and drove out of town. Rumors were that he headed for Vegas with the rest of the money he had gotten for selling his ranch assets. Joe Jr. was not a changed man. He was just settling a score with his dad in the best way he knew. The Mercer Ranch was no longer. Joe Jr. had made sure the entrance had been taken down and burned with the house.

As soon as Anna received the legal documentation giving her sole ownership of the Mercer Ranch, she had every building that was on the property burned to the ground. Then she had the grounds where the buildings had been plowed. She also removed the fence lines that divided the two former ranches. She built new fences on the outer perimeters. She also spoke with the Texas Rangers administration. Together they mapped training courses. Buildings were built for indoor training, complete with a gun range. A bunkhouse was built for the Rangers and a stable.

Anna donated the house on her property built by Joe Sr. to be a safe house for abused women and children. She maintained ownership of the safe house and property on her ranch. She also maintained the house and grounds and paid all the utilities. Cody and Tony were responsible for security at the safe house. Matt and Cord were the physicians for the women and children at the safe house. Anna contacted her sources within the community of abused women and children. They have a very private, very efficient way of taking care of these women and children. All Anna needed to do was make the house available, and the association picked up the ball from there. The house was very secluded, and there were clients that needed that seclusion.

While Anna was busy on The Ranch, Matt returned to his practice. They were still staying together in the same room at The Ranch House. Marion would drive Matt to work and pick him up after work. The time in the limousine Matt used to dictate, prepare for surgery, view pictures before surgery, and develop strategy for upcoming surgeries. The limousine turned into his office. He had always been organized, but this time during the ride, with the quiet of the ride and the solitude, seemed to up his game.

When Matt got home, Anna had his total focus. She was still not able to ride her horses because of her breast healing. She was receiving physical therapy three times a week for her arm. Her arm was still weak, but this last week the therapist measured her progress and had told her he was proud of the strength she had gotten back. It also appeared that she would have a full recovery. Anna and Matt were thrilled that she would regain everything she had lost with her arm injury. Anna took her physical therapy seriously. She did her exercises exactly as the therapist demonstrated and as many times as her therapist told her.

Anna was also busy during the day with The Ranch finances and day-to-day running of The Ranch. Doug came for breakfast in the mornings, especially if there was anything he and Anna needed to discuss. On the weekends Doug and Belle did not come to The Ranch House unless called. The nucleus of their ranch family was Marion, Ben, Jewel, Anna, Matt, and the pair of watchful eyes that were always watching over their safety.

As busy as Anna and Matt were, the upcoming trial of Joe Sr. for the murder of Anna's parents was still in the back of their minds. The district attorney decided after the first meeting in The Ranch attorney's office that the most secure meeting place would be The Ranch. Marion and Ben were the ones coordinating the meetings with the district attorney. The witnesses were being protected. The district attorney suggested relocation for their protection. Cody and Tony found a home and set up the security. The witnesses willingly moved.

Chapter 19

THE SHELTONS WERE HAPPY WITH their relocation. These last couple of years had aged both of them. They had lost their friends after the loss of their oldest son and then the diagnosis of their younger son's cancer. The couples that they had been friends with mainly had sons of their boys' ages. It was very uncomfortable. It proved to be too much to their friendships.

Now the evidence would be presented in court that the Shelton's oldest son, William, was paid to cause the wreck of the car driven by Samson Creed Carter with his wife, Patricia Violet Carter, as a passenger. William had been told it was for insurance purposes. William's parents thought like everyone in the community that it was a tragic accident by a young driver. William was only sixteen.

The Sheltons had decided to clean out William's room and to put their younger son's hospital bed there. The room had a bathroom connected that would also be more convenient for their younger son. While cleaning and making the move, they found a computer chip in an envelope. They recognized William's writing. He had written, "If I die, please view." Both his parents looked at it and kinda laughed. He was a sixteen year old. Why would he write this? When they viewed it, they were sick. William had met with Joe Sr. twice, and both times William had recorded the meetings.

The Sheltons had jumped in the car and drove to Joe Mercer Sr. in prison. The Sheltons decided on the way to the prison that they were not going to tell him about the computer chip. They would just make the accusation. Joe Sr. laughed in their faces. He asked them who they thought had been paying for their young son's cancer treatments. He was paying the bill, and he better not ever hear them accuse him again or he would pull the plug on their son and then he would kill them. He would see to it. Lucky for the Sheltons, they had recorded their conversation with Joe Sr. Their younger son died two months later. That was when they contacted Marion and Ben at The Ranch.

The district attorney felt confident in his upcoming case. He was keeping the information close to his vest. Yes, Joe Sr. was still in jail awaiting trial, but he had done favors for some powerful people in the Dallas area and he might call those favors in to save his own neck.

Joe Sr.'s court-appointed attorney contacted the district attorney for a meeting. The district attorney did hand over as part of disclosures that he had witnesses to conversations and other evidence that Joe Sr. hired a sixteen-year-old child to purposely wreck the vehicle of Anna Violet Carter and Samson Creed Carter causing their deaths. He also had evidence of Joe Sr. threatening witnesses after the fact. The court-appointed attorney was an elderly man who took cases to keep busy after his wife had died of cancer. He was very knowledgeable of the law and had a good practice in his younger days. He had sold his part of the practice to his partner, envisioning an early retirement for himself and his wife. His wife had been diagnosed three months into his retirement. They spent the next two years traveling between treatments. His wife was a very positive person to the end of her life, but it was after she was gone that he had trouble staying involved. He still had his license, and he had kept up his professional insurance. He decided to start defending those in the population that could not defend themselves.

It was very easy for him to return to the practice of law. He had defended several clients, even some he felt were truly guilty, but even those he felt he had gotten them better sentences than they might have gotten without him. Now the court had appointed him to represent Joe Berry Mercer Sr. His first meeting with Joe Sr. left him feeling he had confronted evil and he was going to have to defend evil. Joe Sr. let him know "upfront" that he had ordered the murders of the Carters, but if he had never paid the kid because the kid died in the wreck, it couldn't be murder for hire. The DA had it all wrong, so it should be easy for his attorney to get these charges dropped. Meeting after meeting with his client, he tried to teach him the law, particularly as related to his case. He left telling himself Joe Sr. was a delusional narcissist. He couldn't stand the man, but his job was not to be friends but to give the man the best defense. Mr. Newlin met with the district attorney to discuss the case several times. Then at the last possible minute, still staying within the law, the DA turned over copies of both computer chips to Mr. Newlin. Mr. Newlin viewed the recordings that night, then was first in line to visit his client the next day.

Joe Berry Mercer was advised to make a plea agreement with the DA and avoid the death penalty. Joe Sr. refused. Joe Sr. had decided that if this old man couldn't get him out, he would take things into his own hands. Joe Sr. promised a convict that was getting out on bail payment for them to exchange IDs and let Joe Sr. walk out in his place. The convict told him to let him talk to his wife. He would give him an answer the next morning.

The convict saw his own path to freedom and went straight to call the DA's office. Anything to do with Joe Sr. had gone directly to the DA per his order. The convict got a deal with the DA. All his charges were dropped. They were considered victimless crimes. The sting was set up, and the convict played his role perfectly. He really was a good con; and Joe Sr., being such a narcissist, played right into his hands. The DA got his sound video of Joe Sr., but Joe Sr. was so delusional that even after seeing himself on four separate occasions ordering and bragging about the murders, he continued to think he would find someone to pay off, someone to bribe, someone to blackmail, even Joe Jr. might come back. Didn't they all realize who he was?

Chapter 20

THE TRIAL OF JOE BERRY Mercer began on October 10. Anna, Matt, Marion, Ben, and Jewel sat behind the district attorney. Doug, Belle, and the ten trusted ranch hands sat behind them, taking up the next two rows. The press left one row open behind Mr. Newlin and his client, Joe Berry Mercer Sr. Then they filed in, taking every seat available. The trial was televised on court TV. Joe Sr. insisted the court be open for all access. He knew he would be released scot-free. Who would have the nerve to go against him? He had spent years in this circle. He had information on lots of people. He could still think of things he could pull to get out of this mess, but he wanted his day on national news first. Then he would make fools of everyone, starting with the DA.

When Joe Sr. was brought through the back door of the courthouse. There was no press present. He stopped and asked no one in particular where the press was. He was told they were all in front getting pictures and interviews with Anna Violet Carter. He started mumbling and cursing about Anna ending with words that stopped the guards in their tracks.

Joe Sr. said, "I going to kill her next. I'll make sure she's killed in a wreck just like I arranged for her parents."

One of the guards pointed to his glasses. Only the other guard saw him. He knew his partner didn't wear glasses. He knew he was wearing a recorder.

The DA was all business! He didn't care for theatrics. He had strong evidence, and he led by calling his first witness, the mother of the boy killed in the same wreck. She told about being notified of his death and the grief over his death as well as the grief over her second son's diagnosis with cancer. She concluded her testimony at the point she found the envelope from her oldest son.

Mr. Newlin got up and started forward when Joe Sr. grabbed his arm and said loudly, "She is a damn liar. Don't give her a chance to tell more lies."

Mr. Newlin sat down.

The next witness was the dad of the sixteen-year-old boy. The DA asked him if he was with his wife when she discovered the envelope. The boy's dad began with finding the envelope, then, as questioned, told about what his son had written on the outside of the envelope. The gallery gasped when the dad said, "My sixteen-year-old son had written, 'If I die, view this.'" The DA showed the computer chip, and the dad agreed that was in the envelope. Then the DA walked over; but before he pushed Play, he said, "Your son wrote, 'If I die, view this.'"

There was a black screen, then the sixteen-year-old's face filled the screen. He started speaking.

"Mom, Dad, I love you. Today I took Baby Boy to the doctor. He thought he had an STD even though he is a virgin. Mom, Dad, the doctor told me he had cancer. The hospital business office told me what kind of expenses could be involved in his recovery. I am meeting someone tonight that can help with those expenses. You will understand when you view this video."

The courtroom was quiet as a coffin. The tape showed Joe Sr. throwing open the car door and sitting down in the passenger seat. He outlined how and where the wreck would happen.

The DA stopped the tape. The DA asked the dad if there was another meeting recorded.

The sixteen-year-old's dad said yes. He was talking through the tears streaming down his face. The DA walked over to the recorder and pushed Play. The sixteen-year-old began again.

"Mom, Dad, I love you! I'm beginning to feel like Joe Sr. is not being honest with me. He swears everyone will come out all right, and this is all just about car insurance. Maybe I should not do this. I just don't want Baby Boy to die of cancer." Then he was interrupted by Joe Sr. Joe Sr. gave him $20,000 and said, "I'll pay you the rest after the wreck." Then Joe Sr. started getting out of the car. As he stood up you could hear him say something. It was, "Kill them both."

The DA turned off the recorder and asked the judge for a short break.

The DA, Anna, Matt, Marion, Ben, and Jewel went to a conference room. The reporters ran like their gate had changed at the airport. The judge had ruled on a thirty-minute break instead of the customary fifteen-minute break. This allowed the reporters to make their reports for the noon news.

Mr. Newlin asked his client if he wanted to talk to the DA about a plea deal. He asked his client if the sixteen-year-old misunderstood or loss control of his vehicle.

Joe Sr. said, "I already told you I ordered the wreck that killed them! I made sure that that stupid kid wouldn't chicken out or back off. I made sure his gas pedal stuck."

Mr. Newlin thought he was going to be sick. He stepped over to stand by the trash can. Then Mr. Newlin asked, "What about the $20,000? The money was not found at the scene."

Joe Sr. started laughing. "Stupid kid, it was still in the car. I was the first on the scene and picked it up and put it in my jacket. It was my money."

When the court came to order, everyone was back in their places. Mr. Shelton was still on the stand. The DA directed him through his testimony that after he and his wife saw the recordings they went straight to Joe Berry Mercer in jail.

The dad said, "We recorded the meeting."

This time the screen was filled with both parents and they were saying, "We love you! You have always been a super big brother. We wished we had known how this adult was manipulating you. This is for you!" They went through the prison security and sat down at a table across Joe Sr. Joe Sr. was recorded threatening them not to go to the police. He killed their older son and he could just as easily kill their younger son. He was also saying he was paying for all their younger son's care. If they didn't want his care to stop and stop tonight, they should keep quiet.

The DA asked what he and his wife did next. He told the court they went straight to the hospital to see their son, and as soon as he was asleep, they went to the hospital financial department. Their son was dying, and they wanted to make sure that the grant for his care would continue. The clerk told them that this was her second day on the job but she would see what she could find. She told them after a twenty-minute wait that their son's benefactor was Patricia Violet Carter.

Chapter 21

THE COURTROOM WAS SILENT. THE DA asked for a lunch break. On the hour-and-half lunch break, Anna, Matt, Marion, Ben, and Jewel went once again with the DA to a conference room and lunch was catered. During lunch the bailiff knocked and came in. The DA really expected an offer from the defense. He was pleasantly surprised when he was handed another recording. It appeared to be a video of the defendant coming into the courthouse this morning. The original was given to the court and a copy was kept by the DA and another copy was sent to Mr. Newlin.

When court was called into session. Everyone was on the edge of their seats. The DA finished with the witness. Mr. Newlin was asked if he had any questions for the witness, and he declined. Joe Sr. turned and mouthed to the cameras, "I'll kill them all!" It was chilling for the half of the gallery that saw him do it. A cameraman threw up in a camera bag. Joe Sr. got his sound bite that would live into eternity.

The DA decided not to call the jailhouse snitch as that can put off the jurors sometimes and he had a strong case without it. The next witness called by the DA was an employ of the county as a deputy. The DA skillfully led the questioning until the deputy came to the point that some deputies wore body cameras. Then the DA walked over to the recorder. This time on the big screen was Joe Sr. yelling, "I'm going to kill her next! I'll make sure she is killed in a wreck just like I arranged for her parents." Then the DA rewound the tape to a different point where Joe Sr. is asking where the press is and he is told they are in the front of the courthouse interviewing Anna Carter. Once again the jury and press saw Joe Sr. fill the screen, yelling, "I'm going to kill her next. I'll make sure she is killed in a wreck just like I arranged for her parents."

Mr. Newlin had no questions for the deputy. Or if he did Joe Sr. would not let him cross-examine.

The DA rested his case.

Mr. Newlin had one witness on his list. His client Joe Berry Mercer Sr. Mr. Newlin started to ask a question, but Joe Sr. said he didn't want to be questioned, he wanted to make a statement. The judge asked if he wanted to dismiss his attorney, to which he shook his head no and said, "He is a good attorney. He knows the law. He just doesn't know me! He doesn't know how important I am. I know influential people. This can all be fixed."

The judge ruled Joe Sr. out of order and ordered the jury to disregard his last remarks. Then Mr. Newlin came forward and asked his client how long he had lived in the area.

Joe Sr. yelled, "You know all the answers. Sit down."

Mr. Newlin did just that and turned the examination over to the DA.

The DA began with the tapes of the sixteen-year-old. It was emotional to witness again knowing the outcome. The DA asked one question after each of the two tapes. "Is that you?"

Joe Sr. proudly said, "Yes."

Then the tape of Mr. and Mrs. Shelton was shown. The DA asked again, "Is that you?"

Joe Sr. proudly said, "Yes."

Then the DA showed once again the tape recorded by the deputy. Once again the DA asked, "Is that you?"

Joe Sr. laughed. "Hell, yeah."

The defense rested. The district attorney rested.

In closing the district attorney reminded the jurors for the third time of the videos and the defendant proudly admitting it was him in every video soliciting a child on a suicidal mission to kill two people, then bragging even as he is walking into court that he did it and he will do it again. The DA asked for a conviction on two counts of murder in the first degree.

Mr. Newlin stood up and said he would ask for mercy for his client.

His client stood up and said, "I don't need nobody's mercy."

It was told later that the first vote taken in the jury room was unanimous. The time they were in the room was taken up by answering and filling out all the forms required.

The court was called back to order, and for the count of murder in the first degree of Samson Creed Carter, the verdict was read guilty. The jury was polled, and the courtroom echoed with, "Guilty, guilty, guilty, guilty, guilty, guilty, guilty, guilty, guilty, guilty, guilty, guilty."

In the matter of the count of murder in the first degree of Patricia Violet Carter, the verdict was read guilty. The jury was polled, and the courtroom echoed with, "Guilty, guilty, guilty, guilty, guilty, guilty, guilty, guilty, guilty, guilty, guilty, guilty."

A date was set for sentencing.

Chapter 22

ANNA, MATT, MARION, BEN, AND Jewel thanked the DA and left quietly. Their limousine was at a side door. Once in the limousine it was like they had all learned of the death of Anna's parents. They went straight to the graveside. Anna was distraught. Matt was trying to console her, but everyone was grieving loudly at their senseless loss. Then Wolf came. She sat right beside Anna and howled! It was such pure grief. The wolf pups came and sat beside Matt. They hung their heads.

Anna's life would have been so different if Joe Sr. had never been a part of it. But then she would never have met Matt. After an hour Marion, Ben, and Jewel walked up to The Ranch House together. Anna, Matt, Wolf, and the pups could still be heard sobbing. Wolf had such a human sound to her grieving, it pierced the heart. Jewel cooked. She wanted to make sure she took care of her family. This was the family God had given her, and she loved them dearly.

In the dining room, Marion and Ben talked quietly about Joe Jr. Even though he had not been in court, they were aware he was in the neighborhood. They had learned that he had been staying with the Cruise family. Pamela Cruise was the reason for the first fallout between Joe Jr. and Joe Sr. As far as Joe Sr. was concerned she was not good enough for his son. So Joe Jr. had been sent away to a private school for his senior year of high school. That was when his drinking began.

Now he was back with Pamela Cruise, and it seemed her family had accepted him, even though he was still drinking. Pamela had three older brothers that had rough reputations. The Cruise brothers had an uncle that had done three tours in Vietnam. When he came home, the first thing he became aware of was the gang violence. He decided he would train his younger nephews to defend themselves. While training them, their uncle realized that all three of the brothers never saw a line they wouldn't cross. He tried to instill some type of honor with them, but they made fun and rebelled against any boundaries. Their uncle was very sad and disappointed, thinking maybe he was wrong to have ever trained them.

Pamela had always felt the protection of her three brothers. They were usually close by. But the first time Joe Jr. hit Pamela, none of the brothers were at home. Pamela didn't tell them, mainly because she knew where Joe Jr. kept his money and it wasn't in a bank. Pam was smart enough to never let on that she knew. One night Joe Jr. had been too drunk to drive, but he wanted more Royal Crown. He went to the place where he had hidden the money and got money. He had also been too drunk to notice that Pam was watching him from the bathroom window.

Marion and Ben went back to the family cemetery to check on Anna and Matt. They were all just one ball of fur rolled up together sleeping. Marion and Ben knew that security was always watching over Anna. They slept through the night, then they all came to the back door for breakfast. Jewel was prepared. She fed Wolf and all the pups while Anna and Matt washed up. Everyone was at the dining table and ate like they were home and their favorites were being served.

With Joe Jr. in town, Anna was once again in danger. The security, with the cooperation of Marion and Ben, had been taking care of Anna but Marion felt Anna and Matt needed to be told. After everyone was finished eating and talking over coffee, Marion brought up that Joe Jr. was back in the area. Anna's first thought was that he was here in some way to help Joe Sr. It was decided, whatever the reason he was in the area, Anna was in danger.

Matt didn't want to return to work now that he knew about Joe Jr., but Anna assured him she would stay on The Ranch. She had lots of work that needed to be done. She hadn't told him that her therapist had wanted to see her mount, ride, and dismount her horse. She was so excited. She wanted to surprise Matt.

The days went by swiftly with Matt spending his days at work and Anna spending her days on The Ranch with a therapist. She felt so free now that she could ride again. She loved The Ranch and every aspect of it. She checked the fence lines, she checked all the buildings, and she checked on her ranch hands. She made list of repairs or changes or the need for new construction. She checked her storehouses and got the latest inventory. After the second day, her therapist dismissed her. That evening she went to the third floor to talk to security. She wanted to feel safe, but she wanted to wander around The Ranch as she liked. Cody and Tony agreed. Anna didn't know that they had surveillance in the Cruise home. Pam wasn't the only one that knew where Joe Jr. had hidden his money.

The day of the sentencing of Joe Sr. arrived. Anna, Matt, Marion, Ben, and Jewel once again sat behind the district attorney. The family of Patricia Violet Carter and Samson Creed Carter were not going to make statements at the sentencing. When Mr. and Mrs. Shelton learned that, they followed suit. The only statement made was by the district attorney. He began by saying that the family of the three people Joe Sr. murdered will not be giving statements. They do not want to feed Mr. Mercer's narcissism. The evidence for his conviction of murder they feel defines the sentence of death.

Mr. Newlin asked for mercy. Joe Sr. was sentence to death in the state of Texas.

Chapter 23

T HAT SAME DAY JOE JR. passed out celebrating. Pamela was home with him. She had tried to have at least one of her brothers around when Joe Jr. was drinking. The second time he had hit her, she had gotten into his money while he was passed out. He had over two million dollars hidden. She took $50,000. She decided then every time he hit her, he would pay. She didn't have to wait long. When he awoke on the day of the sentencing, he started pushing her and shoving her. She was afraid for the baby she was carrying, so she finally told him she was pregnant. He was thrilled, hugging her, and kissing her belly. Then all the sudden he flipped like a switch. He started beating her stomach. She started bleeding. She begged him to take her to the doctor. She was having terrible cramps. She tried to walk to his pickup, but he grabbed her again and hit her in the face. Pamela fell to the ground. Joe Jr. started biting her face. She realized he was eating her face right before she passed out. Her older brother pulled up at the same moment. He hit Joe Jr. until Joe Jr. was no longer moving. Then he rushed to Pamela. He couldn't believe how Pamela looked. Her face was in bloody pieces. He lifted her into his truck and headed to the hospital emergency. The police and ambulance pulled up as the pickup pulled away. Anna's security team had called them when they saw Joe Jr. hitting Pamela.

At the hospital Pamela had not been able to tell the emergency doctor that she was pregnant. Pamela was immediately seen by the plastic surgeon on call. While she was in surgery to repair her face, she lost her baby girl. By the time Pamela was out of surgery and placed in a room, the police had arrived to arrest her older brother. A groggy Pamela and her brother had to convince the policeman that her brother had not done this to her. He was innocent. The party was Joe Berry Mercer Jr. The police put out a warrant for his arrest. The charges were murder and attempted murder.

Pamela needed to rest and heal, but she should be able to get pregnant and carry another child. Pamela was in the hospital for three days. Then she was released from the hospital. When Pamela got back home, Joe Jr. was not there. Her older brother went to find her other two brothers in order to go after Joe Jr. She took several suitcases and went to his hiding place. The money was there. She loaded all the money in her suitcases. How much was her daughter's life worth? She pushed her loss to the back of her mind. She drove to an apartment in a high-end neighborhood. They were advertising furnished vacancies. The manager of the apartment complex took one look at her and assured her she was doing the right thing by getting away from whoever hurt her. She paid cash and walked into her new poolside apartment. She put the suitcases under her bed and fell asleep.

She slept for nearly eighteen hours. When she woke up, she went to the nearest furniture store and purchased an apartment full of furniture, including rugs for the wood floors and wall art. It would be delivered in ten days. She was tired, so she went to a drive-through and got food, then went back to her apartment and slept. He texted her brother that she was hiding at a friend's and she was safe. Her brothers were out in the neighborhood and any old haunts of Joe Jr.'s, trying to locate him.

The afternoon Pamela got her new furniture, Joe Jr. was spotted near the old Mercer Ranch. Marion and Ben went out and found him passed out in his red pickup right in the middle of the road. They put on gloves, masks, and rubber boots. Then they approached. He was snoring! They took a knife and cut his penis off and put it in his mouth. They wanted to say, you like flesh, eat your own. But they didn't want to give themselves away. They got in their pickup and drove off.

When they arrived back at The Ranch, they went straight up to security. In security they stripped including their underwear and boots. They took a shower on the third floor, then were inspected and told to go get dressed. Security told Jewel to plan a cookout. They told her they would get the fire going. They used the clothes to start the fire and get it going. Then they put charcoal on top of the burned clothes, got it burning good and put the grill on top and started cleaning it, getting ready for whatever Jewel planned. Marion picked up Matt on time and drove him home. The red truck was no longer in the middle of the road.

When Anna saw the fire, she rushed to see what it was and was pleased they were having a cookout. She loved to sit around a fire and tell stories all night. When Matt arrived, Anna ran to welcome him home and tell him there was a cookout. No one noticed when Tony took two pairs of rubber boots to the hog pen. The boots were extremely muddy when he pulled them up and put them on a shelf with numerous pair of boots that were drying or had been dried after being worn in pig slop.

Jewel started bringing the food out. Once again it was enough to feed the entire ranch. But everyone could have enough to eat and eat again all night. Everyone had made it through dessert at least once when the sheriff's car pulled into the driveway. He got out and came around the house. Jewel insisted he have a plate. He was a good-size man and had a heaping-size plate of food. Wolf was around the fire with her pups. Since they were coal black, the sheriff didn't see them at first.

When the sheriff noticed Wolf, it was because she moved. He really couldn't believe what he was seeing. These wolf pups were on lawn furniture, double recliner to be specific, sleeping all over Anna and Matt. Wolf was stretched out by Anna but on alert.

The sheriff said he hadn't seen Marion and Ben's pickup. They explained they had gotten some supplies and the pickup was in the farmyard. They just left it after they unloaded. Even Marion and Ben were not aware that Cody and Tony had gone over the pickup with a fine-tooth comb and a toothbrush literally. They had hit every inch with a blue light inside and out. There was no blood or DNA to link anyone on The Ranch to Joe Jr. The knife used was completely disassembled and parts were in various ponds on The Ranch.

Before the sheriff left, he told them that this afternoon a young couple had found Joe Jr. in his pickup passed out about two miles north of Anna's property line. Wolf growled.

Anna said, "Wolf knows Joe Jr. hurt me. She knows him and doesn't even want his name spoken."

Jewel said, "Well, Sheriff, is he in jail now for public intoxication?"

The sheriff shook his head and said the couple took him to the hospital. His privates had been cut off and stuck in his mouth.

Anna said, "Well, why? They were useless the way he drank. What do you mean by privates?"

The sheriff said, "His penis."

"Ohhhh" was heard around the campfire.

Matt wanted to know if he was under guard in the hospital. Matt was worried for Anna. The sheriff said there was a warrant served on him for murder and attempted murder. Joe Jr. had beaten Pamela Cruise, causing her child to be stillborn. Then he had started eating her face.

Oh no, Anna wanted to know if Pamela needed Matt's skills as a plastic surgeon. The sheriff said she had been in surgery for several hours.

The sheriff assured them that Pamela had several ruthless brothers. Her older brother was the one who brought her into the hospital. Now all her brothers were together and would ensure her safety.

The sheriff was actually getting sleepy after all the good food. He said his good-byes and also told them all to keep alert. Joe Jr. will be moved to the county jail after the doctors that did his surgery would release him. "Just wanted you to know." He left thinking, had he really suspected someone on this ranch? It obviously was Pamela's brothers that mutilated Joe Jr.

While Joe Jr. was in the hospital, an older man was arrested for public drunkenness. The man was still in the county holding cell when Joe Jr. was transferred from the hospital a week later. The doctors were unsure if he would ever be able to have an erection, but the team of women doctors had done all they could. The second night Joe Jr. was in county jail, the older prisoner jumped up, yelling, "He's trying to choke me. Help me, he's choking me." It appeared that the younger man was choking the older man. He was struggling to get the younger prisoner's hands off his neck. The man was gasping for breath and choking. By the time the county personnel arrived, Joe Jr. was dead. His neck had been broken.

When the older man was questioned, he said, "That prisoner was trying to choke me. I was dying. I guess my military training kicked in. I'm a Vietnam vet." The older prisoner had been in the county for twelve days because he couldn't make bail. He had been a model prisoner. The other prisoners questioned said that he had been defending himself. They saw the guy choking him. The Vietnam vet went before a judge, and the judge ruled the Vietnam vet innocent due to self-defense, and the older man was released. The man walked out of county jail and got into a pickup driven by the oldest Cruise brother.

Chapter 24

THE SECOND DAY PAMELA WENT clothes shopping. She bought herself a wardrobe for daytime and one for partying. She bought five swimsuits. When she got home she napped by the pool. Pamela was a licensed cosmetologist. She got her license her senior year in high school. She would probably try to get a job but in a high-end shop that charged more and got bigger tips.

Joe Jr. had been calling her, but she had never once answered. Her phone was ringing now. It was her mom's brother. She answered, and he said, "You're safe. Call if you ever need me." Then he hung up.

That week Pamela's furniture was delivered, and she paid extra for them to move the furniture that she had been renting to an apartment the manager requested. Fifty dollars a month was taken off her rent. The furniture store had offered white-glove service, and she purchased that as well. Within two hours her furniture was in place on her new carpets. Plus her new pictures were hung. Two big-screen TV were hung, one in the bedroom and one in the living area.

She had a real eye for style, and she brought in a decorator to help pick the window coverings. She went very high tech and modern, and two days later, the decorator had everything hung and working. She decided to purchase another phone. She kept her old phone in case her brothers called, but she felt her new life needed a new phone. She was now completely on her own for the first time in her life, and she loved it!

Her bruises were healing, and the stitches in her hairline were healing. Her surgeon had decided that he could close her facial wounds by putting most of the stitches in her hairline, like he would a face lift. She did have several other stitches on her face. She had seen her surgeon twice already since being dismissed from the hospital. She never went back to the hospital. She saw her surgeon at his office.

Rumors swirled around The Ranch community. Pamela was safe, and it seems Pamela's family had settled the score. Ranch security asked to meet with Anna and Matt. When they got to the security room, Ben and Marion were already there. Cody announced that Joe Jr. had been killed in the county jail by a Vietnam vet that was acting in self-defense.

Chapter 25

MATT AND ANNA HAD SO many invitations for New Year's Eve that it overwhelmed Anna. She left Matt to choose. Matt decided they would start their evening early on The Ranch. Anna was on Matt's arm for the evening. She never asked for the plans. When Anna and Matt came downstairs on New Year's Eve, they were met by their circle of family all dressed in gala. The family walked into the ballroom. First Anna and Matt, then Marion, Ben, Jewel, Doug, and Belle. Anna could not believe how the ballroom had been transformed! It was a white winter wonderland filled with all The Ranch hands with their families. Everyone was quiet the minute Anna walked through the door. She was wearing a beautiful white fur cape. Matt was in a black tuxedo by her side.

Matt took Anna to stand in front of the fireplace. Then he got down on one knee and said, "Anna, will you marry me?" The room went up in a roar, but Matt heard her say yes. Then he put a band of diamonds on her finger and said, "I'll love you, forever." To which she answered, "Forever." He stood and they kissed as the music began playing. They danced the first waltz, then the crowd closed in on the dancing floor. When the doors were opened to the adjoining rooms, the banquet began. It was then that Matt took Anna's arm and led her outside to the ranch helicopter on the lawn.

They boarded the helicopter, and Anna recognized the resort photographer as she jumped into the copilot's seat. Anna told Matt over and over how much she loved him and what a beautiful night she was having. Anna was saying how beautiful Dallas was at sunset when she realized the helicopter was landing. It was landing on the top of the medical complex where Matt had his practice. Anna could see people covering the rooftop. The thought quickly flew through her mind, *Should we land? The roof is so crowded.* Then they were stepping out on the roof hand in hand.

They walked quickly to the farther side where all Matt's friends and medical coworkers were waiting. The rooftop had been transformed into a paradise at sunset. Matt took Anna to a spot where the sun was setting behind them. Then he took off Anna's fur and handed it away. There Anna stood in a golden gown at sunset. She was stunning. More than that everyone was stunned quiet.

Matt got down on one knee and said, "Anna, will you marry me?"

Anna said, "Yes."

Everyone cheered and clapped as Matt put another band of diamonds on her finger and said, "I'll love you forever." Anna answered, "Forever."

The crowd cheered. Matt and Anna danced the first dance of the night. It was magical for Matt. Anna was his golden goddess tonight and forever. The dancing continued as the food was served. Matt took Anna to a table, and plates of food appeared before them. Matt insisted Anna eat even though she insisted she was too excited. Matt's friends, now Anna's friends as well, came by their table wishing them everything good in their future. The party was in full swing and would go on past midnight to ring in the New Year. Matt took Anna's hand, and they slipped away to board the helicopter.

They were in the air over Dallas. Anna was looking lovingly at Matt. Matt was looking lovingly at Anna. Once again the helicopter was descending. The dark sky was lit with brilliant stars. Anna recognized this place. It was the home of the Texas Rangers. She could not believe they had been allowed to land. Matt took her hand and led her inside. There was a beautiful party inside. The Rangers in their dress uniforms with their wives and honeys in ball gowns. Anna loved how colorful it all was. When Matt and Anna started across the room, the Rangers came to attention and everyone in the room stood breathlessly still. Then Matt led Anna to stand in front of a beautiful waterfall. Matt got down on one knee and asked, "Anna, will you marry me?" Anna said, "Yes." Cheers rang out in the room. Matt put another ring of diamonds on Anna's finger and said, "I love you forever." Anna answered, "Forever." Anna and Matt led the first waltz of the night. Anna and Matt celebrated with the Rangers until Anna quietly said, "It might be time for us to leave so they can let their hair down a bit." Matt laughed. "Our ride is here." Matt took Anna's hand, and they slipped outside and ran for the helicopter.

Anna thought they must be headed back to The Ranch because of the path they were flying, but they flew over The Ranch House and continued. Anna had always loved the way The Ranch looked from the sky, but she had never seen The Ranch at night from the sky. It was magnificent! The Ranch was God's country!

She closed her eyes, kissing Matt, until she realized that they were landing. Anna and Matt were landing at the safe house. There was a children's carnival going on in the grand room. Everything a child could imagine at a carnival! Anna learned later that everything had been brought in from Oklahoma to maintain the secrecy of the location. Matt took Anna's hand and led her to the stage. The children followed, then Matt got down on one knee and asked, "Anna, will you marry me?" The children remained quiet, waiting. Anna said, "Yes." Matt put a fourth circle of diamonds on Anna's finger and said, "I'll love you forever." Anna replied, "Forever."

Matt said, "Since she said yes, I have a bag of gold for each one of you." He began calling their names, starting with the youngest to the oldest. Each bag was full of one-dollar gold pieces. Then he directed Anna to stand at the door to the gym and told them to line up by Anna just as he had called their names, youngest to the oldest. When Matt came to Anna and opened the gym doors, there were riding toys to fit each child, the oldest getting mountain bikes. The riding toys went from one side of the gym to the other. The children were in awe. Anna started with the youngest, reading the names on the bikes. The excitement grew as the older children started spotting their names. When all the bikes were given out, a mass speedway was organized with three lanes of traffic marked on the gym floor. Red for youngest, yellow for older, and green for oldest. The children were allowed to stay up until midnight, going back and forth between the carnival and the gym.

Matt took Anna's hand, and they ran for the helicopter! Anna and Matt were happy, happy in love. The helicopter landed at The Ranch. Matt took Anna to the back porch. There was Wolf sitting up with her pups sitting up beside her. Matt took Anna over in front of Wolf and got down on one knee and asked, "Anna, will you marry me?" Anna answered, "Yes." Matt put the fifth circle of diamonds on Anna's finger and said, "I will love you forever." Anna replied, "Forever." Wolf and her pups started yelping in excitement, and the ranch fireworks began. It was the New Year!

Matt said, "Forever," and Anna said, "Forever and ever."